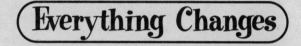

Everything Changes

Other books by
Ann M. Martin

Friends Forever

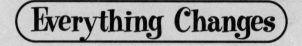

Everything Changes

Ann M. Martin

AN
APPLE
PAPERBACK

SCHOLASTIC INC.
New York Toronto London Auckland Sydney
Mexico City New Delhi Hong Kong

In honor of the birth of
my goddaughter —
Welcome, Harmoni!

ISBN 0-590-50391-X

12 11 10 9 8 7 6 5 4 3 2 1   9/9 0 1 2 3 4/0

Printed in the U.S.A.   40

First Scholastic printing, July 1999

✿ Kristy

First day with this new journal. Am inspired by Mary Anne and all she's been through. Can't imagine losing nearly everything I own in a fire. Can't imagine losing nearly everything I own no matter how it happens. MA is being very brave. She managed to rescue her current diary (the little leather one with the lined, dated pages and the lock and key), which is about her only source of memories these days. Am going to start keeping journals and saving them somewhere fireproof. Think I'll ask Watson if I can put them in his safe.

Have been thinking about the summer, which is going to be an unusual one for my friends and me. Am concerned about the Baby-sitters Club. How is it going to run in July? MA, Abby, Stacey, Claudia, and I will be away for entire month. Jessi, Mal, Logan, and Shannon will be around, but they have so many plans. Logan and Shannon don't usually attend meetings anyway. Have strong feeling that Jessi and Mal cannot run club by themselves. Not sure they'd even want to.

Must think. Is there any way MA, A., St., Cl., and I could run the club long-distance? MA, A., and I will be at Camp Mohawk. As CITs. Have been looking forward to this for SO LONG. Somehow A. and I even wound up in same cabin. Must be fate. Have to say, though, that I wish MA and I had wound up in same cabin. Oh, well. (A. and I will be with 8-year-olds. MA will be with 7-year-olds.)

Will be so great to go to camp again. Can't wait. Day after day of swimming, hiking, softball. Could do without the camp food. Not overly fond of that chicken tetrazzini thing that gets served so often. But do get to eat a lot of ice cream. Also Popsicles. Anyway, do not think we can have much at all to do with BSC while we're busy at camp.

Claud is going off on vacation with family for entire month of July. A first for the Kishis. Cl. does not even know where family is headed. Some sort of big parent-surprise event. Cl. is hoping for beach, of course. Doesn't think she'll be so lucky as to get to go to Sea City (too tacky for Kishi parents, probably for Janine as well), but any beach would be okay with Cl. Most beach towns have plenty of shopping and movie theaters, also min. golf, ice-cream palaces, arcades, and such.

If not beach, then Cl. is hoping for a resort of some sort, but not a spa because food would be far too healthy, and no hope of candy machine right outside hotel room door. Another thought that has occurred to Cl. is a dude ranch. She's not sure what to think of this possibility. In any case, don't think Cl. will be able to do much for the BSC from her vacation spot.

Stacey is off to NYC to spend July and end of June (actually five entire weeks) with father. Of course, she is REALLY looking forward to being able to see Ethan so much. If I think long-distance BSC-running is difficult, can't imagine having long-distance 15-yr.-old boyfriend. (Know Cl. half hopes parents will choose NYC for their vacation spot, but that would be surreal Kishi choice.) Anyway, St. will have five weeks of museums and shows, shopping, eating in fantastic restaurants (prob. no chance of chicken tetrazzini thing appearing on any menu she'll see), and shopping in every store Cl. wishes she could shop in. Do not think St. will be able to do a single BSC-related thing while in NYC.

(Note to self: St.'s mother will miss her very much. Must remind Jessi, Mal, etc. to visit her once in awhile.)

Other BSC members and what they'll be doing in July:

Jess — Dance-o-rama with Mme. Noelle, some sort of special summer ballet program five mornings a week. Will try to squeeze in baby-sitting in afternoons.

Mal — apparently free all summer, but says she's going to write a book???? Will also try to squeeze in baby-sitting, most likely in order to earn money to buy printer paper.

Logan — joined Stoneybrook Baseball League (the Panthers??) and says will be in training for fall football season. Don't know when he plans to squeeze in sitting.

Shannon — actually, haven't spoken to her recently. Must do so before I leave for camp.

Dawn — in CA until August, so entirely out of picture.

Must admit that BSC probably will not run at all while I'm away.

(Note to self: Must phone regular sitting clients

and tell them that in July can call Jessi, Mal, Logan, or Shannon directly should they need a sitter, but not to expect much.)

This is not going to be good for business. Should probably spend several evenings at camp devising ways in which to beef up BSC upon return to Stoneybrook in August. After all, BSC is a gold mine, and I started it. Best thing I ever did.

❀ Mary Anne

Sunday, June 27th

Hello, diary. I'm back again.

It's the end of a VERY hot day. This house does not have air-conditioning. I guess you can't be too picky when the insurance company gives you a furnished rental house (I'm lucky just to be alive), but an air conditioner would be nice.

Today Dad and Sharon and I were feeling the effects of living in such a small house. Once again, I know we can't be picky, but the house is TEENY. Two bedrooms, and I truly believe that mine was originally a closet. (Gosh, these pages are so small and the spaces between the lines are so big. I shouldn't waste words when I write.)

I spent a lot of today worrying that Dad will accept the offer for the job in Philadelphia. I DON'T WANT TO MOVE. All my friends are here in Stoneybrook. I can't help but wonder: Would Dad consider the job offer if our house hadn't burned down? I really feel that he wouldn't, that the fire set in motion some horrible chain of events. I guess that's silly, though.

I hope I don't sound ungrateful, since we did escape unharmed, but, well, first there was the fire, then the possibility of moving, and now this problem with Logan. Ever since the fire he has been so overprotective of me. It's driving me crazy. It's almost as if he WANTS me to cling to him, to need him. And he seems hurt when I don't. But I'm not a clingy, needy baby. I'm doing just fine. How can I convince Logan of that?

I must think. I don't want to hurt him. But I have my life to live. (Thank goodness.)

❀ Stacey

Sunday

Dear Claud,

I know you're still in Stoneybrook, and I'm not even in NYC yet — just on the train. But I wanted to write you a postcard anyway. (Not much room here, so no paragraphs, and teeny-tiny writing.) I am SO loaded down. Packed 4 suitcases, plus one bag of books. Mom had to shovel me onto the train. Can't wait to see ETHAN!!!!! I'll see him tomorrow. Yea!!! Tonight Dad and I are eating at the Cowgirl Hall of Fame. Somehow managed to convince him that eating all the way downtown would be a great idea.

Love,
Stacey

❀ Claudia

Dear Stacey,

Well.

Mom and Dad have sprung thier news. At dinner tonight. They finally told Janine and me where we are going for our vacasion. Is it a dood ranch? No. (Thank the lord.) Is it a spa. Also no, thank the Lord. Is it a resort? No. Is it the beach? Technicaly yes. But I don't think its what I had in mind. We are going to an island. Now dont get to exited. We are not going to barbados or Bermuda or anything like that. We are going to this island off the cost of Maine called Monhegan. I know that is the correct speling because I have a Monhegan ~~brosh bro~~ some Monhegan infomation here on my desk in front of me. It seems to be a very small island only about 2 miles long and 1/2 of a mile wide. It is about 10 miles off the coste of maine. A lot of artists go there. One interesting thing is that several hundred peopel live there during the summer months but only like 75 live there during the winter. Can you belive it. Theres even a one room school house for the few kids who are there in the winter. Most of the poepal who live there all year long are lobestermen. (Mmm. One good thing about Main. I do love lobster. I bet I can eat it every day when we are there.)

Anyway I'm looking at a map of the island and I do see some stores. A Very good sign. And I think some restaurants. Also a very good sign. One of these places in the downtown area of the island MUST be a movie theater. And who ever heard of a sumer vacation spot without minniture golf. I defanitely see an ice-cream stand so all is not lost.

However. Heres the part that scares me. Mom and Dad told Janine and me that the purpose of this trip is a return to the simple life. We are to spend the month reading (worthwile things), hiking, meditatting and so forth. We are staying in a house that belongs to freinds of Mom and dad's. They usualy spend every sumer on Monhegan. (I wonder why there not going this year?????????? Could it be bordom?????) Anyway the house has electrisity (oh my lord, was there a chance it might not???), but it doesn't have a tv, VCR, computter, stereo, or dish washer. Only a radio.

As long as Monhegan has stores and a movie theatre I think I will be ok. Even so I know I will be DESPERATE for news and gossip from NYC so write often. Also I have a huge favor to ask you. Could you please go to the following places for me and then write me about your visits to them? Please go to

— The metrapolitin Musum of Art
— Bloomingdales
— the top of the World Trade Center
— Hard Rock Cafe
— statue of liberty

Even if you just write a postcad about each of your trips that will be fine. But a little more detale would be even better. Stacey I am begging you. Please do this for me. I have never been stuck on a island before.

Stranded (almost),
    Claudia

❋ Kristy

June 29

Have been packing for camp. A long process because every 2 seconds Abby calls. Hasn't been to Camp Mohawk before and keeps wanting to know if has to follow packing list in camp brochure EXACTLY. Have told her it might be good idea. 2 phone calls ago she said, "The brochure says eight pairs of socks. I only have seven pairs. I mean, seven pairs that I like. Do I really have to pack the stretched-out eighth pair?"

Told her yes, that camp laundry facilities are almost nonexistent.

"Okay," she said, and then 5 minutes later called back. "What's a windbreaker?"

"You know, like a light jacket."

"Oh. I thought it was something to do with sailing."

Am a little worried about how A. will fare at camp.

I myself have finished packing clothes and am starting on other items — flashlight, reading material, stamps, bug spray, family photos, and so forth. (Am waiting for A. to get to bug spray on packing list since know it will freak her out.) Really am MORE than a little worried ab

Well, of all nerve. Phone just rang. Picked it up and it was Logan calling to speak to me. Thought maybe he wanted to discuss small surprise he could slip into MA's suitcase before she leaves for camp.

Hardly.

Was calling to (can barely write these words)

Was calling to (maybe will just write words really, really big and get it over with)

HE WAS CALLING TO DROP OUT OF THE BABY-SITTERS CLUB.

Astonishing. Has *no good reason* for dropping out. He is just . . . dropping out. Well, actually, he said he is going to be SO BUSY with sports this summer. Like I haven't heard that excuse from him 10,000 times before. It never prevented him from remaining associate member of club. We lost a full member when Mal went off to boarding school — and didn't replace her. Now are losing one of our backups. Don't know what to think. Could kill L. (not literally, of course).

Wonder if MA knows L. was planning to do this. If she did and didn't say anything to me . . . I mean, I understand about special boyfriend/girlfriend thing. (Thing in which boyfriend/girlfriend always comes first, and you keep secrets from your best friend and your family and everyone for sake of boyfriend/girlfriend. Likewise, when someone tells you something and says, "DON'T tell anyone this, but . . ." you know you have license to tell boyfriend/girlfriend anyway, but no one else.)

Have just reread what I wrote and it barely makes sense. What I am saying is that MA, as girlfriend, prob. knew L., as boyfriend, was going to do this to me, as best friend. Anyway, can't be too mad at MA. Just have to figure out how to replace L. in BSC.

Yikes. A. just called and yelled, "WHY DO WE NEED BUG SPRAY?"

❋ Mary Anne

Hello, diary.

I made a very big decision today, and I know Kristy is going to be mad at me. I decided not to go to camp after all. I feel like everything in my life is so up in the air. I don't know how I could enjoy being at camp when I'd be worrying about Dad and the job and moving. I wouldn't even know where I'd go after camp ends. Back here to the rental house? To Philadelphia? To a new house in Stoneybrook if Dad decides not to take the job? Plus, sometimes I have these terrible nightmares about the fire. I see the flames and think I'm trapped in my room and then I wake up screaming. If that happened at camp, it would be SO EMBARRASSING.

Anyway, at breakfast this morning (Dad, Sharon, and me crammed around the table that folds down out of the wall, as if we lived in a train compartment) I said, "Dad, Sharon, I've been thinking. Would it be okay if I didn't go to camp after all?"

When I explained things as rationally as I could, they said I don't have to go, that they understood.

Result — Dad spoke to the camp director this afternoon. He was very understanding, and said our $$ will be refunded.

Now I just have to break the news to Kristy. And then I guess I'll talk to Logan. Actually, Logan is the one bad thing about staying in Stoneybrook. Do I really want to spend the summer with him? He's SO worried about me that he made the decision to drop out of the BSC without even talking to me first. Once again, trying to protect me somehow. I felt cross about this, then guilty for feeling cross.

❀ Kristy

July 1

What is happening? Don't even know where to begin. Will start with MA.

Well, as it turns out, she DIDN'T know L. was planning to drop out of club. I mean, didn't know until after L. called me. I was all huffy when I spoke to her about it and then SHE got all huffy because L. had made decision without talking to her first. Something is going on between the 2 of them.

Okay. So I am not mad at MA about THAT anymore (am still mad at L., though).

HOWEVER. MA has decided not to go to camp. Can't believe it. Has explained and explained to me why doesn't want to go now, and am TRYING to understand, but don't really. Would think camp would get her mind off worries. Why would she want to moon around Stoneybrook all summer, waiting to see if father is going to move family to Philadelphia? Know she doesn't want to go, but staying home isn't going to help Mr. Spier make decision. And know her house burned down and this is a sad time for her, but again, why stay here and moon about it? Why not go to camp and have fun?

Have been looking forward to camp with MA and A. for months now, and MA is hauling off and spoiling everything.

Hard to believe, but MA's news isn't worst. Jessi's is. J. called this afternoon and we had following conversation:

Me: Hello?

J: Hello, Kristy?

Me: Yes?

J: It's me, Jessi. You'll never guess what.

Me: You sound awfully excited. It must be something good.

J: It is! It's the best! I was at dance class this morning?

Me: Yeah?

J: And Madame Noelle said she had an announcement to make?

Me: Yeah?

J: She said a new ballet program is going to be starting in Stamford. It's, like, a whole new school.

Me: Yeah?

J: It's going to be on a par with the American Ballet School in New York. Those were her exact words. On a par.

Me: Yeah?

J: And she suggested I try out for it.

Me: Cool!

J: It gets even better.

Me: Really?

J: Yes. Madame Noelle said if I get into the program I'll be on the fast track to a professional career.

Me: Were those her exact words too? Fast track to a professional career?

J: Yes! Isn't that exciting?

Me: Definitely.

J: The only thing is that if I get into the program I'll have to leave Madame Noelle's school. So it was especially nice of her to tell me about the auditions.

Me: Yeah, I guess so.

At this point in the conversation there was a slight pause, and for some reason, I was immediately suspicious.

Me: Hello?

J: Oh, I'm still here. Um, Kristy?

Me: What.

J: There is one other thing.

Me: What is it?

J: If I get into the school I'd be going to classes five afternoons a week and on Saturdays during the school year. During the summer, I'd go six days a week.

Me: I guess that wouldn't leave a lot of room for baby-sitting, would it?

J: Not really.

Tried to sound excited for J. Really did. But wasn't. Don't know how well I hid lack of excitement. J. didn't come out and say so, but obviously if she's accepted into program she will have to drop out of BSC. So conflicted. Program would be chance of J.'s lifetime. She deserves it. Would be wonderful for her. But don't want her to drop out of club.

Don't know whether am more upset about MA or J.

Not my best day.

❀ Claudia

Satruday

Dear Stacey,

So far I love this trip!!!!! Best one ever!!!!!! Today we went to freeport!!!!! I have always wanted to do this.

Let me bake up and start with yesterday. We left early in the mornig. Mary Ann came over to see us of. Which I felt bad about. Hear we were driving off on a months vacation and what has her summer been like so far. Well her house burned down, shes not going to camp and maybe her father is going to move her to another town.

Anyway we waved and waved to each other and then the drive to Main began. We drove all the way to Port Land yisterday. Actualy it wasn't a bad drive.

And Port Land is a realy nice city. Our hotel was fine. Not grate, but fine. We didnt spend much time in it. We dumped are stuff in our rooms and went of to explor the city. Guess what I had lobster for diner. So maybe I really can eat lobster every day of this vacasion. By the way it was not a hole lobster it was lobster ~~letta fetu~~ pasta.

Okay, now hear comes the cool part. This morning we cheeked out of the hotel and drove to Free Port. (Its a good thing I didn't know how close we were to Freeport yesterday. I wouldn't have been able to stand the wait.) In less than an hour we started seeing signs for outlet stores. Dad drove us off the highway at the very first Free Port exit and soon we were passing outlet stores left and write. It was astounding. I could hardly contane myself. Dad was good and let us stop at a couple of places but finaly he said, We havent even gotten into freeport yet. Don't you want to spend some time there. It would be a shame to miss the actual town.

Well of course no one wanted to miss the actual town and its a good thing we didn't. In the town the stores were all together in one big hunk. Plus restrants, an ice cream place, and get this — a McDonalds that fetures lobster rolls. I ordered one, so now I am two for two with the lobsters.

Okay back to the shoping. There is so much more than LL Been there. Everything you can imagine plus some stores youve never heard of. One of the best was a store that sells nothing but butons, just rows and rows of boxes of butons. I bought a little bag full to use in jewelry making.

Perchases of the day:

— the butons

— one pare shoes ($3.59)

— one shirt ($8.50)

— souvenears (I can't tell you what or how much they cost because they are for you, kristy ect.)

Biggest disappointment — some of the stores didn't realy have such great disconts.

Favorite purchise — the lobster role.

I hope your having fun in NYC.

More from Monhegan soon.

Love,

    Claudia

❀ Stacey

Dear Claud,

I got your letter two days ago, and this is the first chance I've had to write. I'm so busy here!

Claud, I can't believe the vacation choice your parents made. And they didn't even consult you! A return to the simple life? I have one very important question for you: DOES THE HOUSE YOU'RE RENTING HAVE A TELEPHONE? I'm dubious, since it doesn't have so many other things, including a TV. I mean, not even a stereo? Not even a DISH-WASHER? Well, by the time you get this letter, you'll know the answer to that question. But I have another: WHAT ARE YOU GOING TO DO WITH-OUT A TELEPHONE? Think about it. Let's say you want to order out for pizza. How do you do it without a phone? You'll have to go all the way to the pizza place to give them your order, and, well, that sort of defeats the purpose.

Also, I have been made very nervous by your line about reading worthwhile things. In your case, what exactly does that mean? I suspect it doesn't mean Nancy Drew books, so what is left? Just out of curiosity, what are Janine and your parents going to read this month? And meditating? MEDITATING? What do you meditate about? Have any of you ever meditated before?

I have a very bad feeling about your trip. For that reason, I certainly will write you as often as I can and keep you informed of all details and gossip. Also, I'm going to visit every place on your list. It'll be fun. I'll go with Ethan.

Speaking of Ethan, this is what my week has been like so far:

Sunday — I arrived at 4:00 P.M. and Dad met me in Grand Central. I don't know how he did it, but he managed to hail one of those cabs that's actually a station wagon, and there are, like, four of them in all of Manhattan. Thank goodness he got one, because he and I and all my luggage would never have fit into a regular cab. We rode to Dad's apartment, dropped off my stuff, then took another cab downtown to the Cowgirl Hall of Fame for dinner. I just love that place. Did you know that Chelsea Clinton had a birthday party there once?

Monday — Dad went to work, and Ethan was supposed to go to work, but he took the day off. (The art gallery seems to be pretty flexible about his hours.) We hung out in Central Park — bought pretzels from a vendor, fed the ducks at the lake, watched the Rollerbladers, even went to the zoo. I felt like a tourist. It was great. (Romantic too.) At the end of the day, Ethan wanted to take me to dinner, but then Dad called and said HE wanted to take me to dinner, with Samantha. Samantha is okay, but I would rather have eaten dinner with just Dad. Or better yet, with just Ethan. That would have been a nice way to end our day. Dad and Samantha and I went out, though. This time we ate at Bon 75, a Japanese restaurant in Samantha's neighborhood.

Tuesday — Dad and Ethan both went to work, so I was on my own. Just kind of hung out.

Wednesday — Dad and Ethan at work. In the evening, though, Ethan and I had a real date. He came by the apartment all dressed up and took me to this incredible coffee bar that serves so much more than just coffee. Then we went to the movies. I got home late but discovered Samantha there with Dad, so Dad didn't seem to mind the hour. Ethan took off quickly, though.

Thursday — went shopping in the morning. I need a project while I'm here, since Dad and Ethan are working. (Well, Ethan's hours are flexible, but still . . .) Anyway, I went to a crafts store and looked around for awhile. Finally I decided I'd like to learn how to needlepoint. It must be Mary Anne's influence, and a little of yours. Anyway, I bought a kit to make a glasses case for Mom. (Keep your fingers crossed.)

Friday — started following the directions in the needlepoint kit. Hmm. A little more complicated than I had bargained on. I'll keep persevering. In the evening, Ethan and I went to a party at his friend Mitch's apartment. Mitch's parents weren't there. Got back a little later than I had intended. . . .

And that's the story so far. I promise to write again soon. I'm thinking of you on your desert island.

Love,
    Stacey

❀ Kristy

July 3

Can't believe I am back at Camp Mohawk! Just got here this morning. Already Old Meanie has called for rest period. Thought maybe, just MAYBE, we could have one day with no rest period, but no, Mrs. Means squeezed it in late this afternoon.

Woke up so excited this morning! Feel horrible about L., about MA, about J., but . . . well, it's camp! Called A. first thing.

"Are you all packed?" I asked her.

"Every last thing in the brochure."

"Good." Then I couldn't resist asking, "Even the bug spray?"

"Exactly what kind of bugs are we going to encounter at Camp Mohawk?" A. wanted to know.

"Just the usual. Only larger."

Ate last breakfast with family this morning. Maybe won't miss it as much as thought I might. Was on the messy side. Plus, Karen and David Michael are mad that they're not going to camp this year. Had to listen to endless drivel about spoiled older sisters.

Glad to load trunk into Junk Bunket. Charlie offered to drive A. to bus stop too, but turned out not enough room for two trunks in JB. A., her mom, and Anna met us at high school parking lot. Think Mrs. Stevenson was relieved that A. didn't have to ride in JB in addition to horrible camp bus. When bus lurched around corner, Mrs. S. gasped. But couldn't very well prevent A. from getting on bus when so many other parents were letting their much younger offspring go.

A nice touch — MA showed up to see A. and me off. At first I thought maybe she had changed her mind about camp. But no, she was just there to wave us off. Of course she cried. Of course A. and I did not. Mrs. S. did, though (more at sight of bus bearing down on us, I believe). Don't know what Charlie's reaction might have been. He dropped me and my trunk off, then zoomed away before bus even arrived.

"Later, Kristy!" he yelled. So sentimental.

Got much better good-bye from MA. We hugged and she promised to write, and I promised to write her.

At long last, all stuff safely stored in belly of bus and every last parent had said good-bye to every last kid.

"Kristy, some of these kids are pretty little," A. said to me.

Some of them looked pretty scared too. So A. and I teamed up two of the scaredest-looking kids (7-year-old girls) and sat them in front of us.

"Let's sing songs!" called A. gaily as soon as bus pulled out of parking lot.

Recalled last summer when David Michael had gone to Camp Mohawk too and started singing "A Million Bottles of Beer on the Wall." I tried for something tamer. And shorter.

"How about 'The Ants Go Marching'?" I suggested.

A few feeble voices piped up with, "The ants go marching one by one, hurrah, hurrah."

A. joined in with big, loud voice and soon everyone was singing, even shyest kids. A. is going to do well at camp, I think.

Finally arrived at CM and got cabin assignments.

A. and I and our counselor, Rebecca, walked 8-year-olds to cabin 8-A.

These are our campers:

— Marcia (pronounced Mar-see-uh) Bailey
— Kate Wells
— Harmoni Rose Curtin
— Rachel Werner
— Jenna Front
— LaVonne Simon

Already have bad feeling about Marcia, who is wearing makeup. And not speaking to Harmoni for some reason. A. says to let it go for time being.

Okay.

Must show A. around camp when we have free time. (Next period.) Hope A. will be happy here. Think things are off to good start.

✳ Mary Anne

The Fourth of July

Dear Kristy,

Well, you left for camp yesterday. I've been thinking of you there. You and Mrs. Means and all the campers and counselors, the lake, the arts-and-crafts cabin. I know the arts-and-crafts cabin isn't *your* favorite spot at camp, but it was mine. I bet you're having a great time. I miss being with you guys. But I'm better off here. If I were there, I'd just be worrying about what was going on here.

Today is July 4th, Independence Day. I can smell barbecues. People are having picnics. The fireworks will be displayed downtown tonight. Guess how Dad and Sharon and I celebrated the birthday of our country. We went back to the house one final time this morning and searched through the ashes and rubble. (Isn't it funny that before the fire we said "our house" and after the fire we started saying "the house"?) It was our last chance to do that before the workers come tomorrow to bulldoze the remains.

Logan came with us. Dad and Sharon and I were going to go by ourselves, but when I told Logan what we were doing, he said, "Okay. I'll come with you." Like I had asked him.

I said, "Oh, no. That's okay. You don't have to."

"But I want to. I want to be there for you."

I was thinking that this was a private thing, a family thing, but I didn't know how to tell him that. So I mentioned to Dad that Logan wanted to come with us, hoping Dad would say no, and instead he said, "Okay. That's fine, honey." Which is how Logan wound up accompanying us to the house.

We pulled into the driveway at about 10:30. The second we stepped out of the car, Logan put his arm around my shoulders. You know what, Kristy? I wanted so badly to shrug it off. I want to handle things on my own. I *can* handle things on my own. I'm a very strong person. Why doesn't Logan see that? His arm on my shoulder was like a big sign saying, HERE TO HELP YOU — BECAUSE YOU CAN'T COPE ON YOUR OWN.

Anyway, with Logan's arm still around my shoulders we walked across the lawn to where the house used to stand, to that pile of ashes and bits of wood and metal and who knows what. It was so weird. The fire was several weeks ago and that rubble has been hosed down and rained on and picked through. But we wanted to look through it just one more time. One more time before we couldn't do it again.

I didn't say anything to Logan because I didn't want him to feel sorry for me, but in my mind I was going to search specifically for anything that belonged to my mother. I was wearing that ring of hers the night of the fire, so it's not like I have *nothing* that belonged to her, but so much of her, so *much*, was lost in the fire. All that stuff in the attic — letters, photos, her school papers. Gone.

What I was especially hoping to find was more of her jewelry. In the blue box on my dresser were her charm bracelet and the gold necklace with the pearl pendant. Every time we've looked through the ashes I've searched for those things, but I haven't found them. And so I looked very, very, very carefully for them today. I tried to find other things that might have come from my bedroom and I sifted through the ashes and dirt.

Nothing.

I didn't find the necklace or the charm bracelet or anything else of my mother's. I guess they melted. Anyway, I feel as though I've lost her all over again.

Here's what we did find:

— part of a newspaper (of all things NOT to burn up, imagine, a newspaper)

— part of a shoe

— a cracked dish

— an intact book

— an alarm clock

None of it was worth saving. Even the book and clock had been ruined by water.

As we got into the car to go home, Logan took my hand and whispered to me, "I'll always be here for you, Mary Anne."

I couldn't answer him. I don't *want* him always to be here for me. (Is that a horrible thing, Kristy?)

Write back soon.

Love,
    Mary Anne

�֍ Claudia

Monday

Dear Stacey

I haven't heard from you yet. What's going on.

Well we arrived on Monhegan yesterday. It isn't quite what I expeted. First of all we were led to beleve that theres a town here and there isnt. I just dont understand gidebooks and things like that I really dont. But let me start over with geting to Monhegan becuase it was a nice aventure. There is only one way to get to the island, by boat. We came on a ferry called the Elizabeth Ann the trip took about 50 mins.

We left from a tiny town called Port Clyde. We had to get to the fery really early to be able to load all our stuff on it. Lot's of people were waiting for the ferry. Anyway, guess what there's no bank on Monhegan. Well Mom and Dad knew that but they were surprised to find out that theres no cash machine in port Clyde so what were we going to do about $$$ on Monhegan. The nearest cash machine was in Thomaston and we didnt have time to drive all the way back there before the ferry left. At the last minute Dad got a cash advence on his credit card at a store near the fery dock. I bought candy.

Anyway we finaly got on the ferry along with all these other people and a few pets. The fery was so crowded we couldn't sit down so Janine and I stood on the deck. That turned out to be great. We stared strate ahead and watched Monhegan which is about ten miles away get bigger and bigger. It looked like a huge rock rising out of the ocean. Then we arrived and I just have to say that my heart sank. Where was the town. We stepped of the ferry dock and started up a hill (Someone with a truck was going to bring our suitcases to the house later) and all I could see were a few brown buildings that looked like houses. Well one of the first ones we came to turned out to be a coffee bar, the kind were they sell all different kinds of coffee plus pastries and sandwiches and things. So I felt a little better. Maybe the other houses were realy the rest of the town. Well the next one was a huge hotel. And

Wait I'm going to stop here and tell you about our house first becuse we went to our house befor we explored the town. We walked and walked. As you can imagine there are almost no cars on the island. And finaly we came to a big house with those wethered brown shingels and a sort of sandy yeard. I have to admit that the house is prety in a bleak sort of way.

Then we steped inside. Just like mom and Dad said theres no tv, VCR, dishwasher or stereo. Just a radio. Guess what else theres not one of. A telephone. Can you believe it. If we want to make calls there are a few pay phones on the island that we can use, at the hotels and outside the litle post office. Stacey, is this even safe??? I don't think so.

I hate to admit it but the inside of the house is kind of prety too. Very cozy. I have my own bedrom on the second floor and waht do I see if I sit up in bed. I look right out at the ocean. If I ever wake up early enough I bet I could watch the sunrise form my bed.

Ok back to the town. The truth is there are a few restrants on Monhegan including a pizza place. Also an ice cream stand. But there sort of scatered around, not all together like downtown in stoneybrook. Are you surprised to learn that theres no minature golf or movie theater. Also theres no docter, another thing that doesn't seem safe. What happens if we get hurt. So far I have found 2 gift shops. Very far apart from each other. And a library. And a fish market. And a general store, the only place to buy grocerys. They also sell art supplis and books and things. Well that's it. Mostly what you do here is hike on trails. We have not done that yet. There are 17 miles of trials on the island.

Stacey I am nervous. How am I going to spend a hole month here??? I brought a few books with me, my pastells and paints, a drawing pad, some suplise for making jewlry. Thats it. Mom and Dad and Janine are all happy, talking about the fresh sea air and having time to read or cook or think or whatever. I need a little excitement.

Hmm. Maybe I'll go start a fight over what to listan to on the radio. Then I'll ask if we can have lobser for dinner.

Are you doing all those things I asked you to do? Day dreaming about them may be the most exitment I have here all month.

Love,
Claudia

✳ Stacey

Tuesday

Dear Claud,

I got your letter today. Freeport sounds like a lot of fun. I wish *my* mom or dad would take me on a shopping vacation. I guess you're on Monhegan now. How is it? Do you have a phone? Like I said in my last letter, I bet you don't. How are you coping without it? What are you doing all day long?

Okay, just in case you're suffering from excitement withdrawal, I wanted to let you know that I have begun going to the places you listed in your letter. I started with Bloomingdale's. Ethan and I went on Sunday. As you can imagine, it was not Ethan's idea of a fun and masculine way to spend part of his weekend, but he said he really wanted to be with me.

I wasn't sure this was such a good idea.

"You're going to be bored," I told him.

"No I won't," he replied.

"You were bored the last time we went there. You were so bored you tried on hats in the women's department and embarrassed me."

"I promise I won't do that again. I *promise*."

"Will you bring along something to entertain yourself with?"

"A book. I'll bring a book. And I'll just sit on those couches they provide for bored men. I'll move from Guy Couch to Guy Couch in the store while you try stuff on. Maybe I'll meet some other bored guys and we can talk. . . . What are you going to buy?"

"I don't know. I just want to look."

"How can you do that? Go to a store and just look? I never go shopping unless I need something."

This must be one of the great differences between men and women.

Anyway, we got to Bloomie's early in the afternoon and headed for the shoe department. Ethan had stuck a copy of *Of Mice and Men* in his back pocket. I saw a nice pair of sandals I wanted to try on so I said, "Ethan, I'm going to ask a salesperson if they have these in my size. You go read your book, okay?"

Ethan looked around. He didn't see one of the Guy Couches, only the shoe-trying-on seats. And he wouldn't sit on them because we were in the women's department.

"People will think I'm waiting to try on a pair of pumps," he said.

"You didn't care what people thought when you were trying on women's hats."

"I was in a different mood then."

This did not bode well and I knew it. But I made him sit down and read while I tried on the sandals anyway.

The accessories department was better because a Guy Couch was situated just across the aisle from it. Ethan read — and I bought you a present, Claud! I'll give it to you when we get back to Stoneybrook. It'll be something for you to look forward to this month.

Ethan also managed to find a Guy Couch and read while I tried on bathing suits. But things fell apart entirely when I stepped into the lingerie department.

"There is NO COUCH here," Ethan said in this

incredibly loud whisper, "and I AM NOT going to stand anywhere near all these . . . these . . ."

"Bras?" I said brightly. I smiled at him.

"SHHHHHH!"

"Okay. Go back to the accessories couch. I'll meet you there in ten minutes."

Well, that was the beginning of the end of the shopping trip, Claud. I did meet him back at the couch, but by then he couldn't read anymore. He said he had been too flustered by the sight of all the bras (he whispered the word) to concentrate. So I just took a really long route out of the store and engaged in drive-by shopping as we whizzed past the merchandise. I'll have to go back alone. I want to try on those sandals again, and I saw two great bathing suits (but I can only afford to buy one of them).

I hope this description of my shopping trip lives up to your expectations. Are you entertained?

I promise to write again soon.

Lots of love,
    Stacey

✳ Kristy

July 7

Dear Mary Anne,

Hi! I got your letter at mail call today! I was so glad to hear from you. Now it is quiet time. Remember that? Enforced resting, the perfect time for writing letters. At the moment, Abby and I are in our cabin with Rebecca and our campers. Abby is lying on her bunk reading some soccer magazine. Rebecca is doing her nails. (Her own, I mean, not Abby's.) I like Rebecca. She's okay. She doesn't put up with any nonsense from the kids, and believe me, Marcia can create nonsense. I don't know why she's taken such a dislike to Harmoni. The very second she met her, she just decided she didn't like her. The good thing about Harmoni is that she doesn't care that

Marcia doesn't like her — which drives Marcia crazy.

Anyway, here's what our campers are doing:

Marcia — putting on blue lipstick (she looks like Lily Munster)

Kate — reading

Harmoni — reading

Rachel — writing a postcard

Jenna — staring at Marcia

LaVonne — reading

Abby loves camp. On the first day, when we had some free time, I showed her all around. She likes the playing field and the lake. She desperately wants to ride the horses, but of course that's out of the question. She's hideously allergic to them. And to the hay. And to the manure. Also, she's allergic to most of the trees here. Plus, she's been complaining about the bugs. For an athletic person, she isn't very outdoorsy. Still, there are enough competitive activities here to keep her more than entertained.

Get this: Abby likes the food at camp. Even that tetrazzini thing.

Mary Anne, I'm really sorry you didn't find any more of your mother's things when you went back to your house. I know you have her ring, but still . . . And I'm sorry about you and Logan. I guess he's just trying to be supportive, but he sounds like he's suffocating you. Can you talk to him about how you feel?

By the way, I do know you're a strong person. I've always known it. You may be sensitive, and you may be shy, but you are one of the strongest people I know. Also one of the best.

Okay. I don't want this letter to get too sappy. Quiet time is over anyway. We have free time next, and Abby and I are going to play softball. I can't wait. I'm really having fun with Abby. (But I wish you were here too.)

    Love,
      Kristy

❋ Mary Anne

Hi, diary. It's me.

Well, my grandmother is coming. She called to-day with the news. She says she wants to spend some time with us right now.

Sigh. I don't know how I feel about that. I mean, it's nice of her and all, but sometimes being around her is so uncomfortable. I know she feels guilty about what happened after my mother died, and now that I know the whole story, I feel funny about what happened too. It's not like I blame Grandma or anything. I just feel funny. I was caught in the middle, even though that was so many years ago, even though it was something for Dad and my grandparents to work out.

Oh, I don't know what I'm saying. And worse, I can't stop thinking about Logan. Thoughts about him are swirling around in my head all the time. Why wouldn't they be? He calls me about six times a day — just to see how I'm doing, which is very sweet, but he's driving me crazy.

What I've realized is that by constantly checking up on me, he makes me feel as though I NEED constant checking up on. Which I don't.

An interesting thing is that I resent Logan's rallying around me, but not my grandmother's. I feel uncomfortable about my grandmother's visit, but I don't resent it. And I guess I do resent what Logan is doing.

I wonder if I want to be with Logan anymore.

❋ Claudia

Friday Morning

Dear Stacey,

Finaly I got a letter form you! Thank you!!

Boy are you smart. How did you know we wouldnt have a telephone. You wanted to know waht we're doing without a phone — well, we do alot of walking. Theres no such thing as ordering out. You just go to get what you want and if you have to wait you wait. Or you come back for it.

About our reading. I brought 2 books with me and your right they arent nancy Drew books. I brought a Wirnkle in Time by ~~Mada Madd~~ by ~~Madl~~. Its a newberry winner. I think you recomended it once. And I broght Little woman but it's sooooooo long I dont know if I'll realy read it. But the good thing is that theres a library here I think I mentioned that in another letter which you might or migt not have gotten. Anyway, Mom and Dad and Janine brout all these fancy classical books. I don't know what they are.

About the meditating. I am only pretending to meditat. Whenever were supposed to be meditatting I sit there and write letters to you in my head or sometimes I plan art projets or think about paintings I whant to do. Hey maybe that IS meditating. Who knows.

I am so jealous of you and Ethen and all the time you get to spend together. And of your time there in the big apple.

Well Ill tell you a little more about the iland.

I have to admit that it is one of the most beatiful places I've ever seen. Maybe its THE most beautifull. About the only things here beside the businesses are houses and woods. And cliffs. Well let me describe things to you. You can take walks all across and arond the island to certin points like coves. There are gull Cove and Christmas Cove and Squeaker cove and even deadmans cove. And other places are Burnt Head and Green point and Pebble Beach. Oh I forgot Lobster Cove. And across from the whole island, right where the fery comes in is a much smaller island called Manana. Guess what you can see in the water sometimes. Seals! Can you beleve it. Also there is a fantastic lighthouse kind of in the middle of the island. I forgot to mention that before. And a shipwreck. Now that I think about it theres a lot here besides houses and woods.

Guess what. I have kept up with my lobster recorde. Lobster of some sort every singel day. Yummy delicious.

Now that I have told you how beutiful the island is and whats here and about the lobster and all your going to think I sound spoled when I say the next thing. I am still bored.

I AM BORED I AM BORED I AM BORED I AM BORED.

(Do you think I sound spoilled?)

I think I'm am going to go crazy spending an entire month here.

Yours in bordom,
    Claudia

❀ Stacey

Friday

Dear Claudia,

I think maybe our letters are still crossing in the mail or something, but at least we know they're getting where they're supposed to go.

So you're on Monhegan now. I wish I could stand at the front of a ferry and watch an island that looks like a huge rock rise out of the water. And, well, Monhegan isn't New York, but at least you have that pizza place and the ice-cream stand and . . . Hmm. I'm not so sure about the lack of phone, doctor, etc., but I'm trying to be supportive. I guess you'll just let me know how things go.

Ethan recovered from the trip to Bloomingdale's. (I went back the next day — alone — and bought one of the bathing suits, the cheaper one.) Guess where Ethan and I went the other night. To another party one of his friends was having. Going to a party in the middle of the week, especially a party with no adults present, was just so . . . freeing. Ethan's friend Tomas is older, seventeen I think. Tomas's parents were going to be away for several days, so Tomas invited about ten people over. We stayed up late drinking coffee and listening to the guests read poetry they'd written. It was so cool.

Oh, who am I kidding? It was so boring. But still I felt really grown-up.

The above is the good news.

What follows is the bad news.

I don't know what has gotten into my father, but, well, I think I'll just relate what happened this morning.

Dad was up and dressed and eating breakfast, almost ready to leave for work, when I slouched out of my room in my nightgown, all tired. (Ethan and I didn't go out last night, but I rented two movies and stayed up kind of late watching them.) Anyway, I slid into my chair and just watched Dad eat. I wasn't ready for any food yet. I was barely ready for conversation. But the second I sat down, Dad eyed me and said, "I saw Ethan last night."

This woke me up a little. "You did?" (Dad was out with Samantha last night.)

"Yes. Would you like to guess where?"

I really didn't, but I could tell by Dad's tone of voice that (a) this was not going to be a carefree sort of conversation and (b) he expected me to guess, even though I had absolutely no idea where he had seen Ethan.

"Um, in a restaurant?" I said.

"No."

I realized I was supposed to guess again. "In a store?"

"No."

"Dad, I really have no idea where you saw Ethan. He said he was going to do something with his friends, but I don't know what."

"I saw him," Dad said gravely, "outside the Pony."

"Really? The Pony?" I didn't know what else to say. I mean, so he had seen Ethan outside of some place. So what.

"Do you know what the Pony is?" Dad asked me.

"No."

"It is a club for adults. For *adults*," Dad repeated for emphasis. "Like the Limelight."

"Oh. And you saw him outside of it?"

"Yes."

"*Coming* out of it?"

Dad gave me a warning glance. "No, just standing in front of it."

"Maybe he was waiting for someone to pick him up. Or for a cab or something."

"I hope he wasn't waiting to be picked up at that hour. And he didn't look as if he were hailing a cab."

I tried not to sound as crabby as I suddenly felt when I said, "What are you saying, Dad?"

"I'm afraid Ethan might not be a good influence on you. The Pony is not for kids. It is for adults." (I wanted to point out that he had already said that, but I kept quiet.) "And I don't approve of kids sneaking in."

"But Dad, you don't know that Ethan sneaked in."

"Furthermore," Dad went on as if he hadn't heard me, "I'm wondering if maybe Ethan is too old for you. He wears an earring —"

"Lots of kids wear earrings, kids younger than Ethan."

"Well, I don't approve."

I didn't realize it before, but Dad is so old-fashioned, Claud. Can you believe this conversation?

What a way to start the day. I have a very bad feeling about Dad and Ethan, but I refuse to bring up the subject again. Maybe if I don't mention Ethan, Dad will forget about this. (Although it's going to be hard not to mention him, since we spend so much time together.) I'll keep you posted.

Love,
Stacey

❋ Kristy

July 10

Very pleased with way am keeping up with journal. Write in it almost every day. If our house ever burns down, will have lots of nice memories, as long as journal wasn't in house at time of fire. (Hmm. Must remember to talk to Watson about the safe.)

A. and I having BEST time at camp. SO glad A. is here. LOVE getting to know her better.

This morning, CITs supposed to plan projects for their campers. A. came up with great idea — scavenger hunt. And she came up with good lists of items to find. Somehow, though, activity got off to horrible start.

Divided our kids into two teams. Should have been easy, but right off bat couldn't decide whether to separate Marcia and Harmoni (to avoid problems) or to put them on same team in effort to force friend-ship. A. said forced friendship would never work and that she should know. I said well maybe it would at least force respect. A. just scowled. And in the end, she won and we put them on separate teams. So Team 1 consisted of Marcia, Kate, and Jenna. Team 2 consisted of Harmoni, Rachel, and LaVonne.

"Okay," A. said when girls were lined up in front of us, outside cabin. (Rebecca nowhere to be seen. Whole purpose of this morning, I believe, to give counselors time off.) "I am going to hand out your lists. Study them and ask us questions now, before we start."

Marcia's hand shot up. "Do we get a prize if we win?" she asked.

A. and I glanced at each other. Had not really thought about a prize. "A prize?" repeated A. "Of course." She glanced at me. "Tell them about it, Kristy."

If didn't suddenly like A. so much, would have turned the question back to her somehow. In-stead said, "Abby is going to treat the winners to candy bars from the canteen." (Knew A. could afford this.)

A. scowled again, but what could she do?

Campers were already jumping up and down, examining lists.

A. and I had thought lists fair, equally difficult. But apparently not. First item on Team 1's list — pair of eyebrow tweezers. "Ooh! Ooh!" cried Marcia. "Be right back!" Disappeared into cabin and returned with makeup bag. Hers. Produced tweezers.

"No fair! No fair!" cried members of Team 2.

A. and I looked at each other. Hadn't thought even Marcia would have eyebrow tweezers at camp. So Team 2 hated us until they found extra difficult item on list very quickly and surged ahead of Team 1. As each team worked way down list, became less and less concerned about how other team was doing. Really had fun.

In end, both teams reported back to cabin with completed lists at exact same moment. A. announced that in event of tie, both teams would get prizes, and that she would treat Team 1, while I would treat Team 2.

Hmm. Very tricky.

But still like A.

✻ Mary Anne

July 10

Dear Kristy,

I received your letter this morning. I love hearing about your campers. How are things going now between Harmoni and Marcia? I already like Harmoni, just from your description of her. She actually sounds a little like you. . . .

I'm glad Abby likes camp so much, but I can't believe that she even likes the food. You must be kidding me. (Right?) And I'm glad you and Abby are having so much fun together. Really. I am.

I'm also glad you think I'm a strong person. I have a feeling I'm going to need to be strong where Logan is concerned. Guess what I decided. I decided I have to do something about him, that we can't go on like this. He'll drive me crazy if we do. I almost did something drastic — called him and told him I didn't want to see him anymore. Then I thought things over and realized we need to talk. Logan doesn't even know anything is wrong, and that's because I've just let him call me and hover over me and baby me. I haven't told him he's driving me crazy.

So. This morning I got up my nerve and called him. This was our conversation:

"Hi, it's me." (That was me.)

" 'Morning." Logan sounded very sleepy. I checked my watch. Almost 10:30, but then he tends to sleep late on the weekends. I wondered whether now was the best time to have this particular conversation with him and almost told him I'd call back later.

But then Logan said, suddenly coming to life and sounding concerned, "Are you all right, Mary Anne?"

"All right? Of course I'm all right. Why wouldn't I be all right?" (Don't say anything, Kristy. I know how that sounded.)

Logan hesitated. "Well, I know how difficult this summer has been for you. And now with your grandmother coming and all, I just thought . . ."

"Logan, I'm fine. And in fact, that's what I wanted to talk to you about."

"What?"

"About — that I am fine. I really am. But I feel like you think I'm not fine."

"What do you mean?"

"You're overprotecting me. Or something." Suddenly I felt inarticulate. "You're, um, you're kind of smothering me. And you, um, you kind of seem to want me to need you. To cling to you." There was a very bad silence on Logan's end of the phone. Finally I said, "Logan?"

"Yeah?" (I don't know how he did it, but Logan managed to sound extremely hurt when he said that one word.)

"Logan, I —"

"That's okay. You don't have to say anything, Mary Anne."

"Yes, I do. I — I don't know what I was thinking. Forget I said anything."

"Okay. You want to go to the movies this afternoon?"

And that was how our conversation ended. Absolutely nothing accomplished.

Bravely, but ineffectively,

Mary Anne

Stacey

Saturday

Dear Claudia,

I just wrote to you yesterday morning, Friday morning. Now it's Saturday evening. You won't believe what has happened since the last letter. To give you a clue, I'm supposed to be out with Ethan at this very moment. Instead, I'm sitting in my room writing to you, and Ethan is at home, probably calling all his friends to see if any of *them* can do something with him.

Hmphh.

I had a funny feeling when Dad left for work yesterday morning that I hadn't heard the last about Ethan. I was right. At 11:45 that morning I was sitting in the living room working on that needlepoint thing for Mom. (You know what, Claud? Needlepoint is *hard*. I don't know how you and Mary Anne can do so much knitting and sewing and creating. I had thought I might finish the glasses case in time to give it to Mom when I return from NYC. Now I think I'll have to wait until Christmas.) Anyway, I was sitting there struggling with the yarn when I heard our fax phone ring. At first I wasn't going to bother to answer it because I figured it was just work stuff for Dad. Then I thought MAYBE it was a fun letter or something for me. So I ran to the machine and watched it spit out . . . a memo to me from Dad. He was requesting that I set aside half an hour this evening, from 7:00 to 7:30, to talk to him.

I was immediately suspicious. Why was he being so formal and businesslike? Plus, he knew I was supposed to meet Ethan at 7:00. Plus, we had just had that awful discussion at breakfast. I figured I better say I could meet with him, though. So I faxed him back. I don't know whether he was expecting that, but I couldn't let him be the only one sending faxes. Two could play that game. I asked him if we could set aside a different half hour, the one from 6:30 until 7:00. I figured that way I could be a good girl and go to Dad's meeting, then still meet Ethan.

Dad faxed me back again. (He must have been

having a very slow day at the office.) This is what the fax said:

Stacey —
Meeting to be held from 7:00–7:30. No amendments. Pls. call Ethan and tell him you won't be seeing him tonight.

That was it. That was the entire fax, Claud. It sounds like a telegram, doesn't it? I mean, could it be briefer?

Anyway, I did as Dad requested and called Ethan to tell him we wouldn't be able to get together. Ethan was mad (not at me). I was mad (not at Ethan). I stayed mad for the rest of the day. I was maddest of all when Dad was late to his own meeting. He walked through the door at 7:15.

"The meeting's half over," I announced. I was sitting at the dining room table with a pad of paper, two pens, and a pitcher of water.

"Stacey," said Dad, "this is not a joke."

"I know. That's why I got to your meeting on time."

Dad harrumphed, put his things away quickly, and sat down across from me.

"Shall I take minutes?" I asked.

Dad gave me quite a Look. Then he ignored all my meeting paraphernalia and launched into a talk that he had obviously spent part of the day preparing.

"Stacey," he began, "I've been monitoring the amount of time you spend with Ethan and find that it is way too much."

"But Dad —"

"No interruptions. And you know that I believe Ethan is too old for you."

I couldn't help this next interruption. "He's not any older than me now than he was when I first began seeing him. We age at exactly the same rate."

"Stacey, enough. I just said no interruptions. You're not making this easy on me." (Which was precisely what I wanted.) "I'll get right to the point. You may spend a total of fourteen hours a week with Ethan. That's two hours a day. You may take the time any way you like, but you must, you absolutely MUST be home by 9:30 if you go out with him in the evening."

My jaw dropped. "Now am I allowed to speak?" I asked.

"If you are not going to be impertinent."

"Dad, this is so unfair! Two hours a *day*? A DAY?"

"I feel that Ethan is not a good influence on you."

The conversation went on a bit from there, Claud, but this is the important part of it. What a drag. I'd rather be on Monhegan with no TV.

Your frustrated friend,
Stacey

Claudia

Monday nite

Dear Stacey,

I just got your letter form friday. I have not herd of the Pony either. I think I have herd of the limelite, but I dont realy know anything about it. Are you sure its such a bad thing. Well I guess thats a silly question if it werent a bad thing you're father wouldn't be so upset. But I do think he' is overreacting. So what if he saw Ethan in fornt of that pony place. Like you said it doesn't mean he was IN it.

Boy am I envious. The party at Tomas's place sounds realy cool. (By the way I think you speled Tomas's name wronge.) Drinking coffee and listening to poetry. Very grownup. That sounds like something you'd do on Tv. Does your dad know about that? I think he'd approve. If he knew what you and Ethan were up to maybe he would change his mind about Ethan. I guess you couldnt say that Thomas is 17, though. Or that the party was held at his place while his parents were away.

Well heres what we're up to on Monhegan. Mom and dad and Janine and I are spending lots of time together. We're finding time to do our own things but during part of every day we do something as a family. Yesterday we desided to hike the hole backside of the island. This was realy fun but also a little scary. Listen to some of the things you have to be careful about on this island. No swimming or wading on the back side of the iland because of dangerous undertows. The broshure I got actually says (these are the EXACT words) that no one has been saved who has gone overboard from Green Point to Lobster Cove. Can you believe that Stacey? And the head lands which are like cliffs and are just beautiful . . . well just imagin what would hapen if you fell off cliffs into the sea. And then we went to Gull cove were the broshur says to be really realy realy carful on the rocks becuse their slipery and people have falen into the sea and been lost. Also these huge enormous waves called combers sometimes roll in without warning and (again these are the EXACT words from the broshure) they sweep away anything in their path. Yikes.

But guess what. We had so much fun. It was a great hike and I dont think Ive ever been in such a beautiful place. Stacey, we were high up on the cliffs on the backside of the island and far far belowe us we saw harbor seals swimming along. We all looked at them threw the ~~bin be~~ spyglasses. I have never seen a seal before that wasnt in a zoo. Oh, you have to come hear sometime. Its so hard to describ what we see everyday. Cliffs rising out of the ocean, woods carpeted with pine neddles, lobster traps piled everywhere, boats far out on the sea. Sometimes the fog roles in and everything is all misty and misterious like a Nancy Drew Book.

In case your wondering how I'm am doing with my lobster-eating streek I have not broken it yet. Lobster in some form every single day. Guess how we're going to have it tonight we are going to go to the Fish R Us fish market in town and get whole live lobsters to cook and eat. I plan to disapear when mom has to drop the lobsters into the boiling water. That is so crewel. But I am still looking forward to our lobster cookout.

Love,
Claud

❋ Mary Anne

July 13

Dear Kristy,

I loved your letter about the scavenger hunt! And I can't believe that Marcia has eyebrow tweezers at camp. Does she actually use them? That is kind of weird.

The big news here is that Grandma arrived last night. We were all nervous about her arrival. I mean, Dad has that uncomfortable relationship with her because of what happened after my mother died, and Sharon feels nervous around her because she doesn't know her very well and because of Dad's reaction to her. Also, this is the first time Grandma has been here *since* my mother died, so I thought this might be a very emotional trip, and the last thing we need around here is another emotional person. PLUS, we're so jammed into this teensy house — how are we going to make Grandma feel comfortable here? (She's sleeping in my bed, and I've moved to the pull-out sofa in the itsy-bitsy living room.)

Anyway, Grandma got here at dinnertime last night. She insisted on taking a car service from the airport and wouldn't let us pick her up. At about 6:00 Dad and Sharon and I were in the kitchen putting together dinner when we heard a horn honk. We ran outside and there was Grandma standing by a black sedan. The driver was getting all this stuff out of the trunk of the car — two taped-up cardboard boxes and more luggage than even Stacey travels with. I glanced at Dad and was about to ask him if we were sure how long Grandma was going to stay when she waved to us and we started walking across the lawn toward her.

I have to admit that even though I hadn't exactly been looking forward to Grandma's visit it felt good to hug her. Grandma cried, of course, and said how glad she was to see us. (People say that all the time, but when Grandma said it last night it had special meaning.) Then Dad began to give the driver a hand with Grandma's things. "What did you pack in here?" he asked her with a little laugh.

Grandma shrugged and smiled. "Oh, this and that," she replied.

I glanced at Sharon, but I don't know why. Of course she didn't have any more idea than I did about what was in all those bags and boxes.

A few minutes later the driver was on his way and we were carrying Grandma's things into the house. Grandma looked around our teeny place and said, "Well, this is very cozy." She was being sincere, Kristy. She really meant it.

I looked at our house with different eyes. "Would you like a tour?" I asked her.

"Of course."

"We'll start with my room. We can leave your things in there. You're going to sleep in my bed."

"Oh, I hate to put you out."

"It's okay. This doesn't feel like home anyway."

I don't know where those words came from. They just slipped out. I hadn't meant to say them.

Grandma looked at me gently. "I can understand that, Mary Anne," she said.

I swallowed hard. Then I said, "Well, anyway, this is my room, and over here is Dad and Sharon's room. Back down the hall is the kitchen and across from it is the living room. That's it. Four rooms.

Well, plus the bathroom. Which is right in there." I pointed.

Grandma and I were standing in the living room. "I can see why it doesn't feel like home," she said.

"Yeah. It's furnished with somebody else's furniture. And it's, well, I know this sounds spoiled, but it's just so small. We were used to our old house, where we weren't all piled on top of each other."

"Perhaps it was just that your old house was familiar," suggested Grandma. "It was what you were used to."

I nodded. "I could have gone to camp this summer. And escaped this?" I gestured around at our little house. "I was all signed up. I would have had plenty of space there. But I didn't want to leave Dad and Sharon."

It was Grandma's turn to nod. "Perfectly sensible," she said, and I smiled.

Kristy, I didn't remember that Grandma was so easy to talk to, but she is, and I like that. Now I'm glad she came to visit.

I was going to end my letter here, but I know you too well. You're wondering what I'm doing about Logan. You won't let me get away without telling you. Well, I'm not sure you're going to like the answer. I'm simply trying not to think about him right now. I know I'll have to deal with him eventually, but one thing at a time. Okay?

Lots of love,
Mary Anne

✽ Kristy

July 13

Dear Mary Anne,

What's with Logan? Maybe he's going through that male midlife crisis thing really, really early. He quits the Baby-sitters Club and now he's acting, well, just plain weird with you. So how are things going? Has he let up at all?

Mary Anne, I don't want to be pushy, but I am, and since I can't help it, let me say that you're going to have to stand up for yourself in this matter. Sooner or later you're just going to have to tell Logan what you think, even if you wind up hurting his feelings. I mean, he HAS to hear what you're trying to say to him. And I mean REALLY hear, which means UNDERSTAND you. Am I making my point? I know you already told him that he's overprotective, but clearly he didn't want to hear you. Would you consider writing him a letter? A letter is kind of hard to ignore, with the words written down right in front of your eyes and all.

Okay, enough about that.

Well, one more thing. The next time you try to make a point and Logan doesn't want to hear you and changes the subject and asks you to go to the movies with him . . . DON'T GO!!!

Camp is still great. Do you want to hear about a typical day here? Old Meanie has changed things a bit, so they're different than the last time you were here. Not better or worse, necessarily; just different.

This is our schedule:

6:30 — We're awakened when "Boogie Woogie Bugle Boy" comes blaring over the loudspeaker system. Abby is such a sleepyhead in the morning that I lean down to her bunk (she has the bottom one) and sing along right in her ear, to help the waking-up process.

7:00 — Everyone should be dressed and ready for the day and heading to the mess hall. I walk with Abby and steer her to our table, help her load her plate, etc. She's more helpless than the campers at that hour, but I find it endearing.

7:30 — Campwide meeting to talk about the day: special events and so forth. The counselors sit together at this meeting and leave the CITs in charge of the campers. At this hour, when Abby's eyes are still not reliably open, I consider her one of the campers, so I put myself in charge of everybody.

8:00 — Morning activities begin. Abby and I play softball at some point every morning.

12:00 — Lunch in the mess hall.

12:30 — Afternoon activities begin. Abby and I are in charge of our campers for this next part of the day.

4:00 — Rest hour. You know what that's like. When I'm not writing letters, writing in my journal, or reading, I discuss CIT and BSC activities with Abby. She seems to love helping me make plans and schedules.

5:00 — Free hour.

6:00 — Dinner in the mess hall.

6:30 — Evening group activity.

8:00 — Back to our cabins.

9:00 — Lights-out. (Ha-ha.)

Some of the most fun Abby and I have had has taken place after 9:00 P.M. — telling ghost stories (not too scary) with our campers, planning raids on the mess hall (a little silly since we don't actually want much of what we can find there), planning goofy attacks on other cabins, and so forth. Rebecca is really nice and just sort of closes her eyes when we do this.

Anyway, this is all great, but I miss you, Mary Anne. We're starting to plan Parents' Day, our last day here. When the parents arrive to take us home we'll have a program for them with skits and songs, an exhibition softball game, plus lots of other exhibitions — horseback riding, swimming, archery. If you were here, I know you'd be involved in the arts-and-crafts show. (Neither Abby nor I has been in the arts-and-crafts cabin yet.)

Better go. Rest hour is over and Abby and I are going to go hit a few balls.

Love,
Kristy

❋ Claudia

Tuseday

Dear Stacy,

I know I just wrote to you yesterday, but I whanted to send you this picture of lobster traps. Here on Monhegan the lobster traping season is not in the summer its in the winter. The day the traps go in the water is a very big deal like a holiday.

Oh Stacey I am trying not to be bord but I am anyway. Well I guess the truth is that Im a little lonly. I miss you.

Love,
Claudia

❀ Stacey

Tuesday

Dear Claud,

Following your instructions I went to the Met today! (I went by myself, but that's another story.) I had a great time! It's been awhile since I was here. Do you like this card? I bought it at the gift store. Went to all our favorite spots, starting with the lily pond painting. This month there's an exhibit of early American quilts. They were awesome. I tried to imagine making one of them. (Can't even make that stupid glasses case.) Oh, I wish you were here.

Love,
Stacey

Kristy

July 14

Well.

Of all nerve.

Just got letter from Jessi. Don't even know how to describe it. Horrendous? Stupefying? And yet, for J., good news.

She was accepted into ballet program, the one Mme. Noelle suggested she try out for. I guess I had a feeling that would happen. J.'s so talented. And yet . . . well, maybe will just paste part of J.'s letter down here to document momentous occasion:

Kristy, I have the most amazing news. Last Friday I tried out for the new dance school (it's called the Stamford Ballet Society). At the end of my audition one of the instructors said, "You did a good job, Jessi. You'll hear from us one way or the other in about ten days." Well, guess what. Someone from the school called *yesterday* — just *four* days later — to say that I'd gotten in. They hadn't even seen all the prospective students yet, but they wanted to let me know as soon as possible that I was accepted so I wouldn't make any other plans. That's how badly they want me to join their school, Kristy! Isn't that amazing?

Now comes the hard part of this letter. I've been talking and talking with Mama and Daddy ever since I got this news. Being accepted into the school is going to cause a lot of changes for all of us since I'll be spending so much time in Stamford starting the first week of September. I'll be there until almost dinnertime every single weekday (Daddy can drive me home when he leaves work), and I'll be there all day every Saturday too. That means I'll have only the evenings and Sundays to do my homework. And *that* means, well, I think you can guess what I'm going to say next: that means I have to drop out of the BSC. There's just no way I can remain a member.

Keep reading those last words over and over. *I have to drop out of the BSC. There's just no way I can remain a member.* Bet have read them 50X. What on earth is happening to my beautiful Baby-sitters Club? Everyone dropping like flies. Dawn and Mal honorary members, which means didn't actually drop out but basically are gone. Logan quit. Now J. leaving. Unthinkable. Club is down to five members, plus Shannon as associate, which is joke.

Received letter at mail call this afternoon. Now rest period, and A. is reading letter in her bunk. Am waiting for her comments.

A sad, sad day.

Can't help but think back to when MA, St., Cl., and I first started club. Had no idea what it would turn into. Think of everything that's happened since then. My mom married; MA's dad and Dawn's mom married; D.'s dad married and baby sister for D.; St.'s parents divorced; D. moved back to CA; Mal joined club then left for boarding school; J. joined club, now leaving for ballet school; Mom and Watson adopted Emily; Louie died, then Shannon (puppy) arrived; MA got Tigger; MA got Logan, left L., got him back again, now may want to leave him again; MA learned truth about past and met grandmother; MA's house burned down; A. arrived in Stoneybrook; trips and mysteries and fights and scares. And of course lots and lots of baby-sitting. Remember very first club meeting when we didn't even know St. yet. Remember — wait, A. is calling from below.

Back again. Can't believe A. is entirely supportive of J.'s decision. Says opportunity of J.'s life. Well, it is. *I* know that. But still. A. missing point. Doesn't she see what is happening to club? Had following conversation with A.:

A: Kristy, this is such great news!

Me: I know, but —

A: Not many people get an opportunity like this. Jessi is so talented.

Me: Yes, but —

A: It's so important to follow your dreams. Like, if you discover you aren't happy or find yourself doing things you don't really want to do, then you need to make a change. But sometimes that isn't easy. Good for Jessi.

Me: Yeah. But Abby, what are we going to do without her in the Baby-sitters Club? Logan's gone now too, and Dawn and Mal.

A: Oh, don't worry. We'll manage.

Conversation sort of ended there. Felt as if next words out of A.'s mouth were going to be, "What does it matter anyway?"

Feel depression setting in. Perhaps need candy. More later.

❀ Mary Anne

July 15

Dear Kristy,

Uh-oh, I thought something really great had happened. I thought Grandma had given me courage. See, I've had such good talks with her that I decided to try talking with Logan again. I was going to take the bull by the horns (as Dad would say). I even wrote out what I wanted to tell him and then memorized it. I was going to say, "Logan, we've known each other for a long time now so I feel I must be honest with you. Lately you seem to be smothering me. I know those are harsh words but they're true ones, and nothing is more important than the truth. The thing is, I just can't go on being smothered by you. I'm not a baby and I don't need to be taken care

86

of. I can take care of myself. I'm a strong person."

When I reread those words I realized how they sounded. So then I thought that maybe I could soften the blow by saying them to him over dinner. I thought it would be good for him to hear them in a nice, quiet place, surrounded by one of the things he loves best in the world — food. So yesterday I called Logan to ask him out to dinner.

"Hello, Logan?" I said when he picked up the phone.

"Mary Anne! Hi!"

"Hi. Um, Logan, I was wondering —"

"Yes?" (Logan sounded all excited.)

"I was wondering if you'd like to go out to dinner tonight. I thought it could be a nice Wednesday night activity. We could go to Renwick's and get burgers or something."

"That sounds great."

"Meet you there at six-thirty?"

"Cool."

"Okay, see you."

"See you."

That was our entire conversation, Kristy. I swear. I didn't leave out a single thing. So here's my question. Based on that conversation, would you have thought I was asking Logan on a date?

Apparently, Logan thought so.

When we met at Renwick's he was carrying a little bouquet of flowers for me. I didn't know whether to be pleased or to feel like a jerk. So I settled on *looking* pleased but *feeling* like a jerk. Even so, I decided to go ahead with my plan.

A waitress showed us to a booth and Logan asked her if she could bring us some water for the flowers. I was all set to hold the bouquet in my lap as it wilted rather than ask for such a favor, but the waitress smiled indulgently at us and returned with a tall glass of water. You could practically hear her thinking how cute we were, out on our date.

When she left I placed the flowers in the water, then turned back to Logan. He was smiling sweetly at me from across the table. "Logan," I said, "I asked you here tonight because there's something I have to tell you."

"Yes?" Logan's face softened even further. It was about to melt right off his skull.

"See, the thing is," I began, "um, we've known each other for a long time now, so I feel I must be honest with you."

Logan's face tightened just the teensiest bit at this, but all he said was, "Yes?" again.

"Lately you seem to be smothering me. I know

those are harsh words but they're true ones, and nothing is more important than the truth." Logan was now staring at me from across the table, his water glass halfway to his mouth. I forged ahead. "The thing is, I just can't go on being smothered by you."

"*Smothered* by me?" Logan interrupted, incredulous. And then he said the most amazing thing. He said, "Mary Anne, I thought you asked me out to dinner. I thought this was a date."

"Well . . ." I was about to go on with my speech, but I just couldn't. Logan looked too disappointed. "Never mind," I said. "We can talk about it later. We better look at the menus. The waitress will be back any second."

Logan bent his head to study the menu (which we both knew by heart) and by the time he raised it, the waitress was standing at our table. We ordered, then she brought our drinks, then she returned to say that the kitchen had run out of chicken wings, so we had to reorder, and it took a moment for everything to get straightened out. When it finally did and we were alone again, I looked at Logan and he looked back at me with hurt eyes. I didn't know what to say to him. I couldn't tell him what I needed to tell him, and I found that I didn't have any words to make him feel better. Anyway, if I did try to make him feel better then he would miss the point entirely.

It was a horrible dinner, Kristy. We barely spoke to each other. The moment the waitress cleared away our dishes Logan asked for the check. He paid it, we left. Awful.

Your confused friend,
    Mary Anne

✳ Stacey

Thursday

Dear Claud,

I hope you're sitting down when you open this letter. In fact, if you aren't, go to the nearest chair and sit in it. Seriously. You are not going to believe what I have to tell you. It is very late at night and I'm writing this in bed under the covers by the light of a flashlight. I could probably turn on the lamp because it's so late that I'm pretty sure Dad has gone to bed by now, but I'm not taking any chances. Okay, this is what happened:

Dad came home from work tonight and immediately went out to meet Samantha for dinner. This left me at home to eat dinner by myself. (I suppose I could have called Ethan but we would have had to go out to eat, since I'm not allowed to have him over now unless Dad is here, plus we would have had to be back by 9:30. Anyway, I'm trying to save up my hours with Ethan so that I can see him for big chunks of time on the weekends.) So I ate this paltry frozen dinner and tried to work on that glasses case, which frankly just looks like a mass of yarn and knots at the moment. I figured Dad would be out until at least 11:00, so I was surprised to hear his key in the lock shortly before 10:00. He came in looking all nervous and at first I thought maybe he and Samantha had had a fight. But then he sat down on the sofa, his face serious, and said, "Stacey, there's something I want to talk to you about."

Well, then I didn't know what to think. This didn't sound like a fight. Dad wouldn't want to discuss that with me. Maybe he'd spotted Ethan somewhere else and was going to tell me I was now forbidden to see him. My hands were actually shaking a little as I took a seat in an armchair next to the sofa.

"Okay," I said to Dad.

"Stacey, Samantha and I had a talk tonight," he began, and it was all I could do not to leap to my feet and cry, "Oh, no! You're going to get married!"

Instead, I said calmly, "Yes?" (I actually *was* feeling just a tad calmer, because now I didn't think this had anything to do with Ethan.)

"And," Dad continued, "well, as you know, we've been seeing each other for a long time now."

"Yeah?"

"And we love each other."

"I know."

"And so we've decided . . ."

This seemed to be so difficult for Dad that finally I said, "You don't have to tell me. I know. You've decided to get married. And you want me to break the news to Mom."

"You — ? Mom — ? Oh! Oh, no," said Dad. "No, we've decided to think about living together, about Samantha's moving into the apartment."

I was speechless. I had absolutely no idea what to say to that.

"Stacey?" said Dad after a moment.

At last I found my voice. *"Living together?"* I squeaked.

"Well, yes."

"Here?"

"Yes."

"But Dad, you barely know Samantha."

"Stacey, that's not true."

I knew it wasn't. As Dad said, he and Samantha have been seeing each other for a long time now.

"Well, I don't think you know her well enough for her to move in here."

"How well do you think I need to know her?"

"I don't know. But that's a pretty big step."

"Not as big as getting married, which is what you thought I was going to say."

Dad had a point. But I'm just not ready for any of this, for Dad and Samantha to get married OR for her to move in with us.

"Dad, this is a tiny apartment. There's no room for an extra person here."

"Stacey."

"What."

"You're being unreasonable. You know that, don't you?"

"No."

"Well, anyway, we haven't decided anything yet. This is just something we're thinking about. And I wanted to include you in the decision making."

"Okay."

"Really okay?"

"I guess."

But Claudia, I do NOT want Samantha to move in here. And that's all I have to say about it. (For now.)

Love,
    Stacey

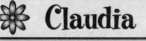

� Claudia

From: CKishi
Subject: Janine brakes rules
To: NYCGirl
Date: Friday, July 16
Time: 8:19:47 A.M.

Hey Stace! Its me Claud. Are you surprize to find this on you're computer. Beleve me I was surprize to find a computer to write to you on. You'll be even more surprized when you find out who this computer belongs to. Janine.

Here's what hapened. Last night we were all sitting around after diner which is what we allways do in the evening. Mom and dad and I were reading. (I was rereading an old papperback Nancy drew that was stuck inside a book I took out of the library here.) Then Janine disapeared upstares. She's been doing that alot lately. Felling like Nancy, I decided to follow her. I just whanted to see what she was up to.

Well my prayers were answered. The door to Janine's room was closed but I herd a faint clicking sound coming form inside. So I did something clever I rapped twice very quickly on her door then just went ahead and opened it like she had told me to come in.

Guess what I saw. There was janine seated on her bed and in front of her was her LAPTOP COMPUTTER. As you can imagine, she definitely was not suposed to have brought it to Monhegan. I wondered how often she had used it. Every night? During the day if Mom and Dad and I were out of the house?

Anyway I was gleeful I ran to her bed and sat on it with a plop. I cried Caught you!

Janine blushed hugely then she began stamering. She didnt know what to say. So I said some things insted. You little sneak! You had your computter all along. You went on and on with Mom and dad about back to nature and evrything and —

Janine shushed me. Keep you voice down, she said. Do you want mom and Dad to hear you.

I think the question is do YOU want Mom and Dad to here YOU?

Look, said Janine. If you don't say anything you can use the computter whenever you want. You can send email to your freinds okay.

Email. Now heres my question if there's no phone here how can we send e-mail. Janin said there are 3 phone jacks in this house. She thinks Mom & dad asked their friends to remove the phones, which means we are only *pertending* to be back to nature. Ha. Ha.

And that is how I came to be seated at a computer on Monhegan, writing you an email. Janine added my name to her acount so you can write back to me anytime Stace. Now we can alway be upto date on our news. No more waiting for letters to arrive.

So . . . write back when you can.

Love,
    Claud

�֍ Kristy

July 16

Dear Mary Anne,

I guess by now you've heard Jessi's news. I mean, I can't imagine that she wouldn't have told you. How exactly did she break the news to you? Was she jumping for joy? Was she squealing with excitement? Was she the least bit apologetic for having to drop out of the BSC? What is happening to us, Mary Anne? One by one, our club members are disappearing. (You're not planning on dropping out for some reason, are you?)

I have to say just one more thing about the club here and then I promise I'll move onto other subjects. The thing is, I understand what a big job belonging to the club is. I really do. You know that there have

been times when I just couldn't juggle everything —
school, homework, activities, and the club. And
every now and then I wish I had more time to devote
to other activities. But then I think about how much
the club means to me. I am so proud of it. It has been
such a big part of my life.

Sigh.

I don't really know where these thoughts are
leading. Just wanted to share them with you.

Okay. On to other subjects.

Last night Abby and I had SO MUCH fun. There
was this party across the lake, a get-together for the
boy and girl CITs. It started when the boys paddled
across the lake in all these canoes glowing with
lighted candles. We girls climbed into the canoes and
the boys took us back across the lake. They were
very gallant. (Don't worry. This isn't as chauvinistic
as it sounds. At the end of the evening, the girls had
to paddle themselves home, and this morning we had
to take the canoes back to the boys' camp.) Anyway,
Abby and I rode in a canoe with these two guys, Jay
and Hal. They were really nice, but . . . DORKY. Hal
kept speaking with this fake British accent that only
he thought was funny, and he spit a lot when he
talked. He was a very moist person. And Jay did
nothing but recite sports statistics. I love sports,

Mary Anne, but I do not need to know 1940s batting averages while being paddled across a lake under a starry sky. Abby and I sat together in the middle of the canoe and tried not to look at each other. Every time we did look at each other we would start to laugh and have to look away again.

Eventually, Jay and Hal got us to shore. We were the last to arrive because the boys were not too adept with the canoe. Twice, Abby and I had offered to take over the paddles, which I know would have cut our time across the lake in two, but the boys kept saying that no, no, they were going to get us there themselves. (Jay actually added, "By hook or by crook," and Hal said, "Righto, gov'ner," and once again Abby and I couldn't look at each other.)

At last we struggled out of the canoe and were back on shore. Abby and I thanked the boys and ran for the party as fast as we could, hoping we weren't being too rude. The party was held under a big tent, which was decorated with lanterns and strings of colored lights. And the food table featured really great stuff — make-your-own s'mores, ice cream, popcorn, chips, cookies. Maybe it doesn't sound like much, but after days and days of mess-hall food it seemed like paradise.

Anyway, kids were dancing, talking, hanging out,

walking around on the shore of the lake. After Abby and I got something to eat we took our food to one of the docks and sat there eating and chatting. A few other kids were already there and after awhile two guys (NOT Jay and Hal) sat down next to us. They said something about the food, we said something about Jay and Hal and the canoe, and before you know it we had introduced ourselves and the four of us were talking away a mile a minute, as if we'd known each other all our lives.

Note: The boys' names were Dan and Barry, and they were not only nice, they were extremely cute.

We sat on the dock with Dan and Barry for most of the evening. When the party ended I suddenly felt all tongue-tied. What were we supposed to do now? We weren't going to see the boys again, and I didn't want some awkward good-bye. Abby saved the day. She smoothly produced a pad of paper, wrote down our addresses for Dan and Barry, and took down their addresses. Then we climbed into a canoe with two other girls, and Abby cheerily called good-bye to the boys. Awkward moment avoided. Abby is the greatest.

More later.

Love,

   Kristy

❀ Mary Anne

July 16

Dear Kristy,

I got your letter this morning. Thank you. I love hearing about camp, the schedule, etc. Our letters keep crossing in the mail. By now you probably already know that I'm trying to work things out with Logan. It isn't easy, though. But enough about that. My last letter to you was all about Logan.

The nicest thing happened this afternoon. Grandma and I were sweltering on our little back porch when I heard the doorbell ring. I ran to answer the front door and found Jessi, Mal, and Shannon standing there. They were holding a large box and they were grinning.

"Hi, you guys," I said.

"Hi," they replied, still grinning.

"Well . . . what's up?"

None of them stopped grinning. "Can we come inside?" asked Jessi.

"Sure, but it's actually cooler outside."

"Really?" Mal looked dubious.

"Really. Over there in the shade."

The four of us sat on these lawn chairs that Sharon had placed in the shade of several enormous oak trees. Then Mal handed the box to me.

"What's this?" I asked. Everyone was acting so strange, like three cats who had swallowed canaries.

"Open it," said Shannon.

I opened the carton and inside I found a large album and all sorts of arts-and-crafts materials. It looked like a very fun box, but I still wasn't sure what it was or what was going on.

Jessi saved me from having to ask too many questions. "It's so you can make a memory book," she said. "See? You can decorate this album, and all the pages in the album, and create new memories."

"All the memories the future is bound to bring," added Mal dramatically.

"Whether you're in Stoneybrook or Philadelphia," said Shannon.

Well, as you can imagine, my eyes misted up. For

a few seconds everything was a big teary blur. "Thanks, you guys," I said. I hugged each of them. They were still grinning away.

Then we dove into the box of stuff. "Look, you can make different pages for different subjects," said Mal. "You could have a first-day-of-school page, a birthday page, a members-of-your-family page, a page just for Tigger."

The four of us plopped down on the ground under the trees and began planning my new memory book. I feel a teensy bit better now. I can't bring back the photos and other mementos I lost, but as Mal said, I can create *new* memories.

If we end up moving to Philadelphia, Kristy, what am I going to do without my wonderful friends?

Love,
    Mary Anne

P.S. Grandma still hasn't opened any of those packages she brought with her. I am getting awfully curious.

❀ Claudia

From: CKishi
Subject: LOBSTER
To: NYCGirl
Date: Saturday, July 17
Time: 9:32:49 P.M.

Stacey are you there. Its me again. I mean its Claudia in case somehow you can't tell. Are you checking your email. Maybe not.

Anyway I have not broken my lobster eating streek yet. The way I had lobster today was GREAT. I have learned something improtent. Its one thing to eat lobster. But the WAY you eat it can realy add to the experience.

This morning dad said What about a picnic lunch?

We all thought this was a good idea but then Janine said What about a LOBSTER picnic lunch. That sounded even better! Here is what we did. Mom and janine ran right to Fish R us and bought four whole small lobsters. They brought them back to the house, cooked them and put them in the frige. While they were cooling, dad and I prepared the rest of are lunch — develed eggs, a fruit salad, and a big thermis of ice tea. Just after noon we set out. We walked along the beach with are picnic until we reached Lobster Cove. Get it? A lobster picnic at lobster cove.

Lobster cove is where the old shipwreck is. We chose a nice flat spot not to far form the shipwreck and spread out are food. Yum. What a feast.

You know Stacey if I had been in Stoneybrook I think I would have been bored the second we finished eating. I mean what else was there to do. You can't swim in the water there and I had forgoten my sketch pad. Everyone else had remembered to bring something to do. Dad and Janine were reading, and Mom was knitting. But you know what I wasn't bored. I just sat on a rock and stared out to sea. I looked for seals. I tried to identafy birds. I've have been looking for puffins but I have not seen any yet. I imaginned how the shipwreck happened.

I dont quite know the words to discribe Monhegan, but they are all good words.

Hey I just thought of something. While I was sitting on the beach thinking and imagining maybe I
was meditatting. I'm not sure. But if thats meditatting its a very nice thing.

What is going on with you and your father and
Ethan now. Well maybe I'll get a leter from you to-
morow. Or a email.

Love You Lots!
Claud

❋ Kristy

July 19

Dear Mary Anne,

I am speechless. I am so speechless that my brain can't even tell my hand what to write. I tried recording this in my journal but I could barely get any words out, so I thought I'd write to you instead.

Mary Anne, there must be something very bad in the air this summer. Or maybe there is bad karma around me. Or I'm giving off a bad aura. *Something.* Because there has to be an explanation for what is happening.

Here is today's bad news.

Abby quit the BSC.

Can you believe it?

I couldn't. Not at first. I thought she was making a very unkind and cruel joke. But she wasn't.

It was our free hour and everyone was meandering out of their cabins, trying to decide what they wanted to do. I was thinking about riding one of the horses, and I called to Abby to see if there was any way she could come along. (So far, she starts sneezing when she's still yards away from the horses.)

"Kristy," she said. "I was about to ask you if you wanted to come with me."

"Where?"

"Down to the dock or someplace. Where we can talk."

Right away I was suspicious. "Talk about what?"

"Well . . . let me tell you when we're all settled. You want a Mars Bar?"

"Not as badly as I want you to tell me whatever it is."

Abby gave me the Mars Bar anyway. Then we decided just to sit on the porch of our cabin. Abby waited until I'd taken a bite of candy. Then she said, "Kristy, I've decided to drop out of the Baby-sitters Club."

I nearly choked. "WHAT?? Why? Why are you dropping out? I hope you have a really good reason!" This is when I briefly thought maybe this was just a bad joke.

"Well, I don't know if you'll think it's a good reason, but it seems like a good reason to me." Abby looked at the ground for a few moments, then she went on. "Kristy, this was a difficult decision for me, but I finally realized that the BSC just takes up too much of my time. I want more time for soccer. And I could afford to spend a little more time on my homework. And I'd just like some FREE time. You know, time to hang out and do whatever I feel like doing. Camp has been so great. I'd forgotten what it feels like to have free time, instead of running from school to soccer to a BSC meeting to a sitting job.

"So anyway I've decided to drop out. It wasn't an easy decision, but it's my final decision."

And that was the end of that. I stood up and left Abby sitting on the porch. I haven't spoken to her since. She is not my friend. How could she be anybody's friend? She's a traitor, a wimp, a bad sport, and extremely lazy.

Love,
Kristy

✽ Mary Anne

Dear diary,

I am so confused. Everything is a jumble in my brain. Dad still doesn't know what to do about the job in Philadelphia, so I feel like I'm in two places at once. Grandma came, which was good. (What is in those boxes, though?) My friends gave me a way to make a memory book, which was great, but now I can't stop thinking of all we lost.

And then there's Logan. He hasn't called since the night of our awful "date." I've tried calling him. In fact, I've called him so often that now I'm embarrassed to call again. He never answers the phone, so I always have to speak to his father or his sister or someone. Or else I have to think of a message to leave on the Brunos' machine. How many times can I say, "Just tell him that Mary Anne called, okay?" or (to the machine), "Hi, Logan. It's me. Again. Give me a call back." Since he never calls back I feel like an idiot.

Now here's the bad part. (I think Kristy would call it the sick part.) Since I haven't been in touch with him, I'm starting to miss him. I keep thinking of what a big part of my life he is. He waits for me at my locker every day. We walk to and from school together. We talk on the phone every single night, even if we've just seen each other. We go to the movies together. He eats half of his meals at my house. We've been on trips together and had adventures together.

I'm lonely without him.

❀ Stacey

From: NYCGirl
Subject: Samantha
To: CKishi
Date: Monday, July 19
Time: 2:57:43 P.M.

Claudia —

I can't believe we can e-mail each other! This is so great! (Bad, bad Janine for sneaking her computer along on your back-to-nature vacation — and yet, good, good Janine. Mentally, I am thanking her.)

I'm sorry it took me so long to get back to you. It hadn't occurred to me to check my e-mail on Dad's computer, but this afternoon I got really bored, so I did. Why was I bored? Because I used up my 14 hours with Ethan over the weekend, and now I won't see him again until Saturday. Does that answer your question, by the way? Nothing has changed where Dad and Ethan are concerned.

Did you get my letter about Samantha? Can you believe Dad's nerve? How could he entertain the idea of her moving in here? For one thing, there isn't enough room in the medicine cabinet for her makeup and stuff.

Write back soon.

Love,
   Stacey

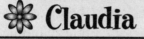

❀ Claudia

From: CKishi
Subject: Monhegans artists
To: NYCGirl
Date: Monday, July 19
Time: 10:31:25 P.M.

Hi Stace!

I'm am so glad you finaly checked your dads computter. And I'm realy sorry about you and Ethen. Have you tried talking about ethan with your Dad lately. Maybe he has changed his mind.

Oh and yes I got your leter about Samanta. Wow there sure is alot going on in you life. Tell me the real reason you dont want samantha to move in it couldn't realy be the medcine cabinat.

Stacey the most amazing thing has hapened since

I wrote to you on Satruday. I've have known for a while that lot's of artists come to Monhegan to paint and sketch. And lots of people who simply like art like me come here to paint and sketch. I mean they just take the fairy over for a day they don't live here. Half the people who get off the farry (their are two farries and they arrive a few times a day) are holding sketchpads. Later you see them walking around sketching. Theirs so much to sketch — the cliffs, the ocean, the sky, the woods, the shipewreck. Then they get back on the ferry at the end of the day and leave.

But what I just found out today is that lots of serious artists live here all summer. One of them is Charles Martin well he's not alive anymore but he used to have a house here and come to Monhegan sumer after summer. He drew cartoons, and he ilustraited several books for children plus he did beautiful pantings and drawings. Theres a whole exibit of his work here.

Thats not all. I discoverd that some of the artists who live here open there studeos and you can walk around the iland and tour the studeos. You can watch the artists at work or view there work or just talk to them.

Thats what I spend yesterday doing. I went by myself. I just went form studeo to studeo. I looked at so many wonderful paintings and sculptures. It was like living in a musum. Some of the artists were busy so I didnt talk to them, but I talked to about four others. They shared their work with me and asked me what kind of work I like to do. And this one REALY cool artist her name is Rachael Mann (I know thats speled right becuase she gave me her card) we talked for ONE HALF HOUR. She talked to me like a adult.

Monhegan is a wonderfull place Stace.

Your exited friend,

Claud

❀ Kristy

July 20

Dear Mary Anne,

It's been more than 24 hours since Abby gave me her news. I've managed not to speak to her since then. This has not been easy. When I first left Abby (sitting on the porch with her mouth hanging open) she ran after me.

"Kristy? Kristy?" she kept saying. But I just walked faster and faster until she had to run to keep up with me.

"Aren't you going to say anything? . . . Kristy? . . . Are you ignoring me?" (Duh.) "Kristy, this is so juvenile." (Well, I certainly wasn't going to answer her if she was going to say mean things about me.)

Abby tried once more. "Kristy? . . . Kristy? . . . KRISTY!"

We had reached the softball field by then and lots of kids were milling around, including several of our campers. Abby didn't want to make a scene, so finally she left me alone. Since I wasn't responsible for our campers at the moment, I stalked off to the edge of the woods so I could think in peace. I sat under this big tree until dinnertime. In the mess hall I positioned myself as far from Abby as possible — not an easy task since we have to eat at the same table, but at least we sat at opposite ends of the table and on the same side, so it was hard to see each other.

The evening group activity was relay races and I made sure not to be on Abby's team. Afterward, back in our cabin, I simply refused to speak to her. At lights-out, for the first time since I arrived at camp, I actually got into bed and went to sleep.

When I woke up this morning, I found a note pinned to my blanket. I knew it was from Abby, so I unpinned it, threw the pin down onto her bunk, crumpled the paper, and threw it away. When "Boogie Woogie Bugle Boy" came on I let Abby go on sleeping, and I managed to get out of the top bunk without disturbing her. She was awakened later by Marcia leaning into her face and calling her an ir-responsible CIT. Ha.

Anyway, I could go on and on, Mary Anne, but you get the picture. It is now 8:45 P.M. We are in our cabin. I am lying on my bunk writing to you. Everyone else is writing a song. (Our campers decided we should have a special 8-A song, about what a great cabin we are.)

Here's how many times Abby tried to speak to me today: 14.

Here's how many times I answered her: 0.

Now she seems annoyed with me. Well, it's good for her. I'm annoyed with her. Beyond annoyed. Furious. Beyond furious. (What comes after furious? I don't know. But whatever it is, that's what I am tonight.)

How could I have thought Abby was my friend?

So tell me — what's going on with you and Logan? Have you managed to have The Talk with him yet?

Love,
    Beyond Furious Kristy

❀ Mary Anne

Tuesday, July 20th

Good evening, diary,

I had such a nice talk with Grandma tonight. I realized something — she's the perfect person to talk to because she's a newcomer. That didn't come out right. She's good to talk to because she's an impartial party (just had to go look that up). That's what I mean. Impartial. Sometimes it's hard to talk to my friends about Logan or about moving, because they know Logan, and because of course they don't want me to move. So we have these very one-sided conversations. On the one hand, my friends are saying all the things I want to hear. On the other hand, this isn't very helpful.

So anyway, I talked to Grandma about some of

this stuff tonight. Grandma doesn't have a stake in any of it (well, except that she wants me to be happy). That means we have more realistic conversations. I started off talking about the idea of moving. (I couldn't quite bring myself to discuss Logan with her. I just don't feel comfortable yet talking about my boyfriend with my grandmother.) Anyway, Grandma was great. She asked me to tell her all my fears about moving. Then she asked me to tell her the good things. That took me by surprise. I had thought there weren't any good things, but as soon as I started thinking, I came up with a few. Now I feel sort of relieved.

Hmm. Maybe tomorrow I WILL talk to Grandma about Logan.

Good night, diary.

❀ Stacey

From: NYCGirl
Subject: Samantha (again)
To: CKishi
Date: Tuesday, July 20
Time: 9:15:47 P.M.

Hi, Claud —

No, the medicine cabinet isn't the only reason Samantha can't move in. There's also the matter of the closets. They are all already stuffed and there are no spare coat hangers. So it's entirely out of the question.

That is so cool about Rachael Mann and the other artists!

More later.

Love,
    Stace

❀ Claudia

From: CKishi
Subject: Mom brakes rules
To: NYCGirl
Date: Tuesday, July 20
Time: 11:22:39 P.M.

Stacey you just wrote to me a couple hours ago. I know this becuase I swiped janine's compputer to tell you this most incredible news, and I checked my email before I started this letter to you.

This is the incredable news. Not only did Janine brake the rules but now mom did too. I was just about to go to bed tonight. It was kind of late and dad had alredy gone to bed. I went downstares to say goodnight to mom. She was in the living room and she was reading something. She was concentratting so hard she didnt hear me until I was right next to her. When she looked up and saw me she jumped and stuck her book under the couch cushin. I dont know what came over me but I reached right under that cuchion and pulled out the book it was one of those harlaquinn romances! She found it here in the house. I remerber when she first found it she said it was trash not the kind of reading that will expand you mind.

Ha ha, I cried!

First I caught Janine and now mom. I won't let mom forget this!!!

Stacey you can BUY more coat hangars.

Love,
   Claud

❀ Stacey

Wednesday

Dear Claud,

How do you like this postcard? I'm at the last place on the list of places you wanted me to visit — the Statue of Liberty. I mean, I'm actually right AT the statue, standing near its base. It is so impressive and imposing. I think I might go to Ellis Island next. (The ferry stops there before returning to Manhattan.)

I LOVED your e-mail from last night. I can't believe your mom! I wish I could have seen her face when you caught her. I hope you were gentle with her, though. Because then you could remind her of that the next time *she* catches *you* at something.

Love,
Stacey

July 22

Dear Kristy,

I just got your letter and decided I better answer it right away. I CANNOT BELIEVE that Abby dropped out of the club too!!

I have to say that although I was surprised Logan hadn't told me about his decision to drop out of the BSC, I *wasn't* surprised that he was dropping out. And I wasn't surprised that Jessi dropped out either, not after her news about the dance school. But Abby? Wow.

Are you sure you should be quite so mad at her, though, Kristy? I don't think that's a good thing. After all, Abby isn't doing this to hurt you. She's doing what she feels she needs to do. Just like when I felt I needed to stay home this summer and not go to camp. You know, that decision wasn't easy to make, and I bet Abby's wasn't either. I hope I don't sound like I'm lecturing you, because I don't mean to. It's just that you and Abby are pretty good friends now. Are you sure you want to spoil your new friendship? Maybe you should talk to Abby. I feel a little funny giving you that advice, though, since you told me to talk to Logan, and I haven't managed to do that. At least, not properly. We still haven't spoken. On second thought, ignore my advice. No, wait. Don't. You HAVE to talk to Abby, Kristy. (Well, maybe you already have. Your letter is from three days ago. A lot could have changed since then.)

The news from here is that Grandma finally revealed the contents of all her parcels to us last night. She made a big production out of it, which was fun. At dinner she said that if we had time, she wanted to make a presentation to us that evening. I saw Dad and Sharon look at each other, exchanging a glance that was puzzled and intrigued, which was exactly how I felt.

"What kind of presentation, Grandma?" I asked.

"It's a secret. I can't tell you until we have gathered in the living room. Perhaps with ice cream?"

That sounded good to me. Ice cream and a mysterious presentation.

As soon as dinner was over, Dad served up four bowls of ice cream that he brought into the living room on a tray. Grandma had disappeared, but a few minutes later she showed up carrying two of the parcels. She made another trip for the rest of them. When she came back, she set them on the coffee table and said to us, "I know you've been wondering what on earth I carried here with me from Iowa. I think it's time to show you. They are some things that belonged to Alma."

To my mother? I felt my heart begin to pound.

I looked at Dad. He had loved my mother fiercely. What must he be thinking? We had both lost her twice — and now here she was again. Or at least little parts of her life.

Grandma went on. "You lost everything you owned in the fire — heirlooms, photos, letters. Obviously, I can't replace the things that were lost, but I wanted to give you some other things. I want you to know that you didn't lose all that remains of Alma. Just the things *you* had."

Dad's eyes had filled with tears, and Sharon reached for his hand. We watched as Grandma used a pair of scissors to cut through the tape she had sealed the largest box with. When she finished, she lifted the lid and started removing items. Each was wrapped in tissue paper. First came a photo of Mom on her wedding day. It was a portrait photo.

"That's — that's," I stammered. "I remember seeing a photo just like that in our attic."

Dad smiled a tiny, embarrassed smile. "It was only in the attic because —" he started to explain to Grandma.

But she waved him away. "It's okay, Richard," she said. "No need for excuses." She said it kind of brusquely, but I think it was just because her eyes had filled with tears as she removed the tissue from the photo.

Next Grandma unwrapped a small silver cup and a dented silver ring. "Your mother's first cup and her teething ring," Grandma said to me. I heard a small gasp and looked at Dad, but it was Sharon who had placed her hand to her mouth.

Grandma pulled out parcel after parcel, and as she did so the four of us moved around the room in an unhurried dance. Dad sat next to Grandma for awhile, reading through a box of letters Mom had written Grandma and Grandpa when she was away at college. Then I squeezed between them to see a dress Mom had made for her Barbie doll (it was horrible, Kristy!). Then Grandma moved next to Sharon and opened a box of Mom's artwork from grade school and they looked through it together.

I watched our dance and gazed hazily at what Grandma had brought. We didn't lose everything after all, I realized. Little bits of Mom's history were here, in our hands, before our eyes. And, Kristy, this sense of calm began to settle around me.

I watched Grandma and Dad and saw that they seem to have a new understanding of each other. Did it take a FIRE to destroy the bad feelings between them? I don't know. I don't like to think so. The fire has changed too many things. But I do realize now that it didn't destroy everything. We have one another, of course, and we even have Mom back again.

I am beginning to feel a tiny bit hopeful, Kristy.

Lots of love,

Mary Anne

✳ Claudia

Friday

Dear Stace,
I have so much to tell you that I desided to write you a reglar letter. An email would tie up Janines computer for to long and I don't want to get caught, especialy not after I cuaght mom. I want to look like the good girl for as long as posible. I think that will come in handy one day.

Well the exitement mounts. My lattest discovary is that not only can you visit the artists in their own studeos, but some of them give art classes that people who visit the island can sign up for.

Guess how I fond out about this. Rachael told me.

Guess why she told me. Becuase she's teaching a two day class and she asked me to sign up for it. (I did.)

Guess who else signed up for the class (Prepare yourself). Janine. I am not kidding.

Gues who talked her into it. Me.

I just thought it would be fun I thought it would be somthing nice we could do together. I mean neither Janine or I has any friends here, and Janine has been realy nice about leting me use the computter. And plus I really like the fact that she defyed Mom and dad and brought the computter in the first place.

When I mentioned the class to Janine she got all nervouse and said Oh no I cannot do anything like that. I said, But it will just be for fun. She said No your the one whos good at art Claud. I said Anyone can be good at art Janine. (I didn't mean it but I realy wanted janine to try the class.) Finaly she said she would sign up so we ran over to Rachael's studeo (no phone remerber?).

The first class was held yesterday, and the second one just ended now. Stace we had so much fun!! I wasn't realy sure what to expete with Janine I have never taken a class with her. I thought maybe she might get all bossy or try to teach the class. Then I thought maybe if it turned out that she wasn't very tallented she might try to cover up by lecturing the other students about famouse artists or somthing. But no. In fact I saw a side of janine I havent seen before.

Let me start at the begining.

At 10:00 yestruday morning Janine and I showed up at Rachael's studeo which is a cabin in the woods. Everything is all hushed as you walk along. If you listen carfully you can hear birds and the ocean but it all seems sort of distante. Then you enter the cabin and sudenly your surounded by easles and paints and wonderful arty smells. And there was Rachael. She was talking to two other woman and a man but when she saw me she smiled and waved. Afew minutes later she came over to speak to us.

This is when I frist saw the other side of janine she said all flustery, Hi I'm Claudia's sister and she's the one who knows everthing about art. I don't know anything. I can barely draw a stick figure. I hope your expetations for me aren't teribly high.

Rachael smiled and pated her arm. She said that if Janine had fun expresing herslef in the class then that was all that matered.

Janine looked unsure.

Afew minutes later the class began. There were

8 of us, mostly women. I was the youngest. Rachael began by demonstratting and talking about some technikes. Then she let us experamant with water colors and oils. (This was a beginers class Stacy, but I had lots of fun anyway.) That frist day we worked on a still life of some fruit that was in a bowl in the middel of the room. I set right to work. I knew I wanted to try my hand at a still life that looked like Salvador Dolly might have panted it. But Janine was all seriouse, and slowly began working at her picture, fruit by fruit. She was so intense. She kept saying, Oh this does not look right Claudia. It doesnt look like fruit at all. She was all mathodical and painstaking. But you know what the more Rachael and I complamented her on her fine job the more she loosened up.

The next day we took our easles outside and panted in the woods. When Janin saw me set up to paint this one tree, and then saw me start off with purpal pant on my brush she sudenly brightened. Oh I get it, she said. You dont have to pant realistacaly. And from then on she just sailed. She realy got lost in her work.

You know what? In the end she had a very nice sort of free panting but better yet she said she had had so much fun and that she found the experiance very mind expanding!!!

I hugged her.

Oh, I just love Monhegan Stacey. This is the best place in the world.

Love,
   Claud

Kristy

July 23

Cannot abide Abby. Is inconsiderate, immoral creature with tiny, tiny mind of plankton.

Ways to torture her:

1. Switch bunks with Marcia.

2. Arrange for Jay, Hal, or both to show up and announce they have evening off, intend to share it with A.

3. Wait until A. has just finished brushing teeth, then say, "Oh, is that your toothbrush? I used it to clean the toilet. Sorry."

4. Tell Old Meanie that A. loves getting up early and should be put in charge of playing "Boogie Woogie Bugle Boy" every morning.

5. Tell cook to serve A. ONLY tetrazzini thing.

6. Sign A. up for all book and record clubs can find. (This falls into category of ways to torture A. should it become necessary to continue torture after return to Stoneybrook.)

✿ Stacey

From: NYCGirl
Subject: Kitchen table
To: CKishi
Date: Saturday, July 24
Time: 4:12:51 P.M.

Dear Claud,

Just thought of one more reason why Samantha really can't move in with us. Our miniscule kitchen table is barely big enough for Dad and me, let alone a third person. We'd have to pull out the side in order to accommodate her, and when you do that you can hardly move around in the kitchen.

So once again . . . out of the question.

Love,
    Stacey

✱ Claudia

From: CKishi
Subject: Rachael Mann
To: NYCGirl
Date: Saturday, July 24
Time: 9:52:46 P.M.

Hi!!!

Stacey. You can fold the side down when your not eating meals then you can still walk around the kitchen.

You know, I dont want to be pushy or anything but are you realy giving your father a chance. Are you being fair to him. He loves Samanta and I bet he's lonely when your not there which is alot of the time. Also he didn't come to you and say, Stacy I have made a decision. Samantha is going to move in with me. He said What would you think about it. Also he said that he and Samantha are *only* thinking about it. He's trying to include you. Well I gues if it were my dad I might fell different.

Anyway.

Rachael's art class is over, but I keep going back to her studeo. Rachael is so nice. I brought her a batch of sketches I've done on the island and she looked threw them realy carfully. She comented on each one and she said I have alot of talent. (Oh I just love hearing that!!!!!)

Gues what. When I went to Rachael's today she said, Claud I was just about to take my sketch pad to the cliffs do you want to come with me.

Well of course I did we had to go back to my house frist so I could get my own pad and tell Mom and dad where I was going to be. Mom and Dad got to meet Rachael then and they realy liked her. (Janine was all shy arond her. I mean Rachael is JUST SO COOL.) When I had my pad and box of pencils and charcoles we walked across the island to the cliffs. Then we sat in the sun looking out in different directions. For the longest time we didnt speak we just sat and thought and sketched.

Stacey you know that was one of the most peaceful times I can ever rember. The sun on my shoulders, the waves braking far below, a seal or two, gulls calling, and my sketchpad in front of me. You dont get quiet like that in Stonybrook you just don't. Oh I think I could live hear forever.

Right now its dark of course and the fog has rolled in. I have grown to love the fog. Its so enveloping and in a way comforting.

I don't like to think about the fact that we will have to leave hear soon.

Love,
Claud

✿ Mary Anne

July 26

Dear Kristy,
    GREAT, GREAT NEWS!!!!!!!!!!!!!!!!!!!!!!!!!!!!!!!!!!!
!!

Dad came home from the office tonight and something about him looked a little different. Sharon was already home from work and she and Grandma noticed it too. We all stared at Dad for a moment and then Sharon said, "What is it, Richard?"

"Well," Dad began, "I've been talking to the people in Philadelphia."

"And?" I said.

"Well, I want to see how you feel about this, but I've decided I'm not interested in the job. It's not right for me after all."

"YESSSS!!!" I shouted.

Dad grinned at me, but then he said, "Sharon? What about you? The courses you wanted to take in Philadelphia?"

"Well, I can't take them in Stoneybrook, that's true, but I'm sure I can find something in Stamford. Maybe I could even go into New York City once a week."

"Mary Anne?" Dad said, smiling. "I take it this is all right with you."

I threw my arms around Dad and gave him a gigantic hug. And Sharon said, "Let's eat out tonight. To celebrate."

"To celebrate being Stoneybrookites," I said.

So now, Kristy, we can start looking for a new house in Stoneybrook. We won't have to live in the rental for much longer. This is so exciting! Where do you think we'll end up? Back in our old neighborhood? Closer to downtown? I really don't care as long as it's in Stoneybrook, and as long as we have a little more room than we have right now.

Oh, Kristy, I can't wait for you to come home from camp!

All right. Now I have to make one teensy confession. And I don't think you're going to like it.

This is it:

One little part of me is almost disappointed that we're staying here.

Guess why.

Because if we had moved to Philadelphia I would have left Logan behind — and our problems as well. I wouldn't have had to deal with them, and now I do.

What does that mean, Kristy? It can't be good.

I know, I know. I have, *have*, HAVE to talk to Logan. But I've already tried, and look where it's gotten us. We *still* haven't spoken. If I try again and it doesn't work for some reason . . . well, then where are we? This is so confusing.

I'm glad you'll be back soon. I need to talk to you in person.

Love,
    Mary Anne

✿ Stacey

Tuesday

Dear Claudia,

Oh. My. God. You won't believe all that has suddenly happened in the last few days. It began on Sunday, when Ethan and I were spending one long delicious afternoon together. We were walking through Central Park, even though the day was hotter than blazes. We were just walking lazily along, chatting. Out of the blue, Ethan asked me about Dad and Samantha, whether they'd made any decision about Samantha's moving in.

"No. Thank goodness," I answered.

Ethan gave me a funny look. "Why do you say that?"

"What?"

"Why do you say 'Thank goodness' and sound so aggravated?"

"You know why."

"You know what? I don't. Not really. I don't understand why you're so opposed to the idea."

"Well, I — " I began to say.

"I really think you should be more open-minded about it, Stace."

"I'm a very open-minded person!" I exclaimed.

"I don't mean to sound harsh, but you're NOT being open-minded at all. Not about this. Which is kind of ironic, considering that we were saying how closed-minded your father has been about me."

I started to say something, then stopped. In fact, I stopped altogether; stood stock-still on the path we were taking through the park. "You're right," I said after a minute.

"I mean, is there a REALLY good reason you don't want Samantha to move into your dad's apartment?" Ethan asked.

"No. I guess not. I — it just would have been a big change, that's all. I'm not used to having Samantha around so much." Ethan looked at me with a little half smile. "Okay, okay. That's a terrible excuse," I admitted.

All afternoon I thought about what Ethan had

said. The first thing I did when I got home that evening was ask Dad if he had time for a talk. He did, and I told him I had changed my mind about Samantha, and how that had happened.

"Ethan said those things?" Dad asked. I nodded. "Well, he sounds very sensible."

"He is. He's a good person to talk to."

"He sounds very mature too."

"Is that good?"

"Of course."

"But I thought you said Ethan was too old for me. And that that was why you wanted to limit the amount of time we could spend together."

"There's a big difference between age and maturity," was Dad's response.

I had to think about that for a long time, Claud. This is what I've decided it means: that anyone can be old and do things that come with being older, like voting and driving and getting married and having kids. Or drinking and going to clubs. But not everyone can do those things with maturity. You could be 35 but an irresponsible drinker or an irresponsible parent. Now Dad has seen that Ethan is not only older but mature. (Well, he hasn't actually SEEN that yet, but I know he's gotten a sense of it from the things Ethan said to me.)

Today Dad called me from the office to see how I was doing. I was working on that needlepoint thing, Claud. You will HAVE to help me with it when we're back in Stoneybrook. You simply won't believe what it looks like. Do you think it's supposed to have knots on the front? Anyway, I told him I was fine and that I'd been thinking over what he had said last night.

"Ethan really is pretty mature, Dad."

"He certainly sounds so."

"Then do you think maybe I could see more of him again?"

"I'd like to get to know him a little better first. Then I'll make up my mind."

That sounded fair. "Okay," I said.

"Maybe you and Ethan and Samantha and I could have dinner together before you go back to Stoneybrook."

It's a good thing we were talking on the phone and not in person, because when Dad said that my eyes practically bugged out of my head.

I coughed. "Dinner?" I managed to say.

"Just the four of us. So we can get to know each other a little better."

I tried to picture Dad and Ethan engaged in sparkling dinner conversation. Then I tried to picture Samantha and Ethan engaged in any kind of conversation. But finally I managed to croak, "I'd like that."

"Let me look at my schedule and talk to Samantha and we'll see if we can find an evening this week when the four of us could go out."

"Okay," I said in a small voice.

And so . . . we are going to have dinner on Thursday. Keep your fingers crossed, Claud. Maybe your toes as well. And could you cross your eyes?

Love,
Stacey

❀ Claudia

From: CKishi
Subject: Dad brakes rules
To: NYCGirl
Date: Tuesday, July 27
Time: 1:46:26 P.M.

Ha ha ha, hee hee hee.

Stacey, now Dad has broken the rules!!!!! I am the only one in my family who hasn't broken the rules. Well exept for using Janin's computer but I wouldnt have done that if SHE hadnt brought it along. Can you beleve it. *I* Claudia Kishi, the one who didnt want to come on this vacation in the frist place, the one who didn't know about meditatting and didnt want to go back to natur — I am the one who has done the best job at it.

Are you wondering what dad did. Well it was great. We were finishing lunch on our deck about an hour and a half ago. We were having leftover lobster salad (No I still haven't broken my recorde yet — lobster everyday.) As we were finishing Dad stood up and stretched very casaully and said I think I'll go next door and see what the Rubens are up to. (The Ruben's own their house, Claud. They spend every single summer here. We've have gotten to know them a little.)

I helped Mom and janine with the dishes and then I thought maybe *I* would see what the Rubens were up to too. So I ran across thier lawn and I was just about to knock on their door when I heard a noise from inside. It was a nose I hadnt heard in a long time. It was the nose of a tv.

Hmm I thought, this is very strang.

I dont know what got into me then Stace, but insted of knocking I quitely opened the door and tiptoed inside.

Well.

Not only was dad sitting there watching a game on Tv, but the Ruben's werent even home.

Dad!!!!! I cried.

Claudia!!!! dad cried.

It was some moment.

I allmost ran back to our house and dragged mom and Janine over to look at dad, but then I re- merbered Mom and the romance book. I figured I had earned afew points then by not telling on Mom. Now I could earn afew more by not teling on dad. And you know me, I can allways use points, es- pecally once school begins.

So finally I said to Dad, Well I gues I never saw this. You were over here to look something up in the Rubens encyclapodia, right.

Dads red face began to die down a little. Right, he said.

Then we went home.

I am so proud of myself, Stace.

Whats going on with Ethen and Samanta.

Love,
    Claudia

July 27

Have been thinking things over and have decided maybe shouldn't be mad at A. anymore. Must be big. Must be mature. Can't understand why anyone would drop out of BSC for no good reason, but still want to maintain friendship with A. Really. Have been remembering all fun things A. and I have done together, and not just this summer at camp. Have been on school trips, coached soccer games, gone to parties and sleepovers. A.'s bat mitzvah was very special weekend. Will never forget it. Plus A. is just all-around nice, funny, caring person. Must not lose sight of that.

Oh, who am I kidding? Haven't been big at all.

Didn't come to this conclusion on own, by any stretch of imagination. First, campers came to me all upset and said wanted A. and me to be friends again. Very important to them. Then — very, very bad — A. found list of mean things I wanted to do to her. Had decided list wasn't nice thing to have in journal, so had ripped out, crumpled up, and thrown away. But somehow A. found it (suspect Marcia). Then

Hmm. Better back up and start at beginning. Campers came to me yesterday after quiet time. A. had just left cabin to go for swim. Campers started to go with her, then circled around, came back to cabin, and trapped me. Were SO upset about A. and me. LaVonne was actually crying. Didn't want to see us fighting. Two good things came of this. 1. Realized how childish have been and decided to talk to A. ASAP. 2. Campers were united — all of them. Even Marcia and Harmoni. The six of them were drawn together by common disillusionment in me. Nice to see united front.

But felt awful about causing their unhappiness.

At any rate, knew had to talk to A. Went looking for her at lake. Couldn't find. Returned to cabin. And there was A. in empty cabin — reading crumpled-up piece of paper from journal. (*Know*

Marcia responsible. Hope only did it to help force reconciliation between A. and me.) At first wasn't sure what A. was doing. Then she looked up, saw me, and said didn't know plankton had mind, not even tiny, tiny one.

Think I blushed. Or turned pale. One or other. Then started stammering. A. didn't make things easy for me. Sat on bunk with paper in lap and stared at me, waiting for me to stop stammering and actually say something. Stared at me for about 30 seconds. Finally, I said, "Guess where I've just been."

"So you're speaking to me again?"

"Yes. Guess where I've just been."

"To the plankton store? To see if they carry larger minds?"

"Abby, I'm sorry. I'm really, really sorry. I was just at the lake. I was looking for you because I wanted to apologize to you."

"Are you sorry about the size of my brain?"

"I'm sorry for all the things I said to you and did to you, and especially for not respecting your decision to leave the Baby-sitters Club. I don't exactly understand why you're dropping out, but I don't want to lose you as a friend because of it."

A. relaxed. Almost smiled. "Really?"

"Yes." Told her what had changed mind. We talked for bit, then A. gave me huge hug.

A few minutes later, went off in search of campers to show them we were friends again.

Now am happy, happy, happy.

✳ Claudia

Wenesday

Dear Stacey,
One last lobstar postcard before we have to leave the iland. Can you beleve the month is allmost over. We leave hear in two days. I think you leve NYC pretty soon too so I'm am sending this to Stonybrook.

Guess what I have fallen in love with Monhegan. I want to come back evry summer. Every singel summer of my life. Maybe one day I will live hear but I guess the winters are pretty hard.

Stacey I don't want to leve. But I do want to see you.
Love,
Claudia

✿ Mary Anne

Dear Kristy,

I am mailing one final letter to you, hoping you'll get it on the last day of camp. You can read it on the way home. (If it arrives after you leave, will the camp forward it to you? I hope so.)

Once again, I have SO MUCH news! Everything is happening so fast. It's kind of overwhelming. Where to start? Hmm . . .

Well, I'll start with dinner two evenings ago. We were eating out because it was Grandma's last night here. I had dreaded her visit, Kristy, and by the time she had to go home, I didn't want her to leave. She made the visit so special. I'm starting to feel like my old self for the first time since the fire.

Anyway, we were at The Country Mouse, and just after the waiter had cleared away our plates and was about to serve coffee, Grandma reached into her purse and pulled out a tiny box. She handed it to me.

"What's this?" I said.

"Open it."

I opened it. Inside was a gold ring. I looked at Grandma. "Did this belong to my mother?" I asked.

"No," she replied. "But it was going to. It's mine. It was given to me by my mother, and I was going to give it to your mother, but I didn't have the chance. So now I'm giving it to you."

Oh, Kristy. This has been such an emotional summer.

Grandma left yesterday morning. She cried. I cried.

Then last night, Dad and Sharon and I were about to start dinner when Sharon said, "Let's go out again."

It was 93 degrees and we were roasting. Plus, nobody felt like cooking. We went to Friendly's, partly because it isn't too expensive and we've been eating out a lot lately, and partly because the air conditioners in there are always going full tilt. So we were sitting around drinking iced tea and waiting for our food to arrive when Dad said, "I had an idea at work today."

"You did? What?" asked Sharon.

"Well, I know it sounds crazy, but do you think our barn could be renovated?"

"Renovated to LIVE in?" I asked.

"Yes," replied Dad.

We all looked at one another. It WAS a crazy idea. I mean, it would be a big, huge, ENORMOUS job, but . . .

"I think it could be done," said Sharon.

I don't know why we hadn't thought of this before. We still own the property, Kristy. And the barn wasn't damaged by the fire. It makes perfect sense if you think about it.

"What about simply building a new house where the old one was?" asked Sharon.

"That's as big a job as renovating the barn," said Dad.

In the end, we all decided we liked the idea of living in a barn. So that's what we're going to do. Of course, it will take awhile, so today Sharon was going to start looking for a house for us to rent in the meantime. (We simply can't stay in the rental we're in now; not for a year.) But guess what. Before she could even call a realtor, the phone rang. It was Mrs. Hobart. And you will never, ever, ever guess what she had to say.

Mrs. Hobart was calling because she had heard that we had decided to stay in Stoneybrook and she wanted to tell us that the Goldmans' house is for rent. The GOLDMANS'!!! Right next door to Claudia's. Mrs. Hobart said she wasn't sure we'd be interested because the Goldmans are renting their house out for just a year. They've decided they might want to move to Florida now that they've retired, but they aren't sure, so they thought they'd rent a place down there for a year on a trial basis. And they'd rent out their house in Stoneybrook at the same time. At the end of the year, if they want to stay in Florida, they'll put the house on the market. If they don't want to stay, then they can come back to their old house.

That arrangement works out perfectly for us! We'll live at the Goldmans' for a year until the barn is ready, and then the Goldmans can either sell their house or return to it. And meanwhile, I'll be living on our old street again, right next door to Claud!!!!!!!!!!!! If this were a newspaper headline, it would read: MARY ANNE SPIER RETURNS TO

BRADFORD COURT. "SHE'S GIDDY!" SOURCES REPORT.

Isn't it funny the way things work out?

I'm going back to the street where I grew up.

Even though this means a lot of moving around — from the rental house to the Goldmans' to our barn-house eventually — and a lot of work to do on the new place, I'm excited. And I'm so, so happy. I wouldn't say this has been a great summer, but maybe it will end well.

Call me the second you get home, Kristy. I can't wait to talk to you.

I MISS YOU!!

Love,
Mary Anne

✿ Stacey

From: NYCGirl
Subject: My Dinner with Ethan (and Dad and Samantha)
To: CKishi
Date: Thursday, July 29
Time: 11:25:52 P.M.

Dear Claud,

I have a feeling this is my last e-mail to you in Monhegan. Tomorrow you leave your island, and I leave mine (Manhattan, that is). I'll be home by lunchtime, but I think you return on Saturday. Anyway, I figured I could send you one last message and fill you in on The Big Dinner, which took place this evening.

Guess what. It was not a disaster. In fact, it went pretty well, considering that I was ridiculously nervous. Dad had said I could choose the restaurant, but I thought it might be better if he chose, so he did. (I figured that if anything went wrong, at least it couldn't be blamed on my choice of a restaurant.) Dad settled on a French bistro just a few blocks from our apartment. We walked inside, then through a shuttered door and found ourselves in this delicious garden behind the restaurant. We were right in the middle of the city, but we felt as though we were in the French countryside. I tried to relax. Then I told myself that if I were really in France I would be excited, not nervous. But I couldn't think of a single thing to be excited about.

Anyway, one of the best things about the evening was that because it was still almost 90 degrees when we arrived at the restaurant, everyone else was eating indoors with the air conditioner, so we had the garden to ourselves and weren't hot at all, thanks to a lot of fans. When we had been seated and served drinks (iced tea for Ethan and me, white wine for Dad and Samantha) this hugely uncomfortable pause followed, during which I obsessed on Ethan's earring and hoped Dad wasn't doing the same thing. Then all four of us started to speak at once. We laughed and Dad said, "Ethan, I'm glad you could join us tonight."

"Thank you, sir," Ethan replied.

Dad beamed. He loves being called sir. (I relaxed a teeny, tiny bit.)

It took awhile, but eventually we got around to the tough subjects of Ethan and me, and Dad and Samantha. At one point, Ethan boldly said, "I didn't want to get involved in something that wasn't really my business, but I did tell Stacey that I thought she ought to have an open mind about Samantha. I mean, my mom and dad are still married so I don't have any experience with this kind of thing, you know?" (Dad winced ever so slightly at the "you know.") "But I still think you have to at least entertain all sides of any issue."

Now, Ethan is smart; I know that. But I had never heard him talk quite like that before. I think I was gazing at him with my mouth ajar. Dad's mouth was closed (so was Samantha's), but I could tell he was EXTREMELY impressed, maybe even more impressed than I was.

The result of the dinner? Dad told me I can now see Ethan whenever I want, within reason. (Oh, goody, he says that on my last night here.) And

Samantha said she's still only THINKING about moving in with Dad, but that my respect for her decision makes the decision-making process easier. I like that. I like that Samantha cares what I think. That means SHE respects ME, doesn't it?

So . . . what happened after you caught your dad? I want to know details. I guess I'll have to hear them when we're back home. Can you believe our vacations are over? We looked forward to them for so long, and now they're almost behind us.

Have a safe trip!

Lots of love,

Stacey

�֎ Kristy

July 29

Wow. So many mixed feelings.

Is very late at night, long after lights-out, and for once campers are asleep (at least, think they are). Can't sleep myself, though, so pulled out flashlight and journal.

We're down to final end-of-camp activities. Strange, because isn't REALLY end of camp, just of our session. By Monday, another session begins. But feels like end of camp. Tonight was special after-dinner activity, which will describe in moment; tomorrow is rehearsal for skits for Parents' Day; and next day, Sat., is Parents' Day — which means we go home. (Sad face.)

Back to this evening. So glad A. and I have made

up. Campers thrilled as well. Even Marcia and Harmoni still getting along. H. said didn't want them to end up like A. and me. Hmphh. Not sure want to be that kind of example. Anyway, for last week, each cabin has been preparing a skit or song or dance routine to put on this evening. Our girls wrote skit entitled "Peace and Harmoni." (Guess who came up with title.) All about getting along, fights, making up. Was hilarious. Marcia and Harmoni decided to play each other. Had fine time. Marcia lent Harmoni all her makeup, and was very good sport when Harmoni went overboard and wound up looking like someone arrested by Cover Girl Police.

Will include excerpt from skit here:

Marcia (playing Harmoni): La, la, la, la, la. Oh, I just love camp. Everything here is so wonderful.

Harmoni (playing Marcia) enters wearing all her hideous makeup.

Marcia: Except for the Forest Monster.

Harmoni: Forest Monster? What Forest Monster?

Marcia: Oh, it's just you, Marcia. Please forgive me.

Harmoni: I never forgive anybody for anything.

Marcia: Let's not fight. Let's ask our CITs to help

us work out our problems. Kristy, oh, Kristy. Could you come here for a second?

LaVonne (playing me): Certainly. Let me just finish writing this nasty note about Abby in my private journal. Okay. All done!

Marcia: Kristy, why would you write something nasty about Abby in your journal?

LaVonne: Because Abby is a pigheaded —

Jenna (playing Abby): Excuse me! Excuse me! I heard that. And Kristy, you are —

Marcia: Well, Marcia, I guess our CITs are not going to be able to help us.

Harmoni: Maybe we'll have to help them.

Skit went on from there. Was a little embarrassing but not too bad. Most of audience was laughing. Think A. and I laughed hardest of all. Sat together during evening and thoroughly enjoyed performances. Think is great sign of maturity when can laugh at self.

Wait. A. is whispering to me from below.

Okay. Back again. Is now almost an hour later. A. climbed up here for late-night chat. Tried again to explain to me decision to drop out of BSC. Told her she didn't have to do that. Said felt compelled to. Said is happy we're not fighting anymore, but would be even happier if I actually understood her decision. And now I think I do.

A. said she loves baby-sitting and especially loves belonging to BSC. Feels thankful to have moved to new town and found so many great new friends so quickly. Knows she's lucky, that that doesn't happen very often. But went on to say she's beginning to feel overwhelmed. Stretched too thin. There are just not enough hours in day to fit in everything she wants to do, and now the regular meetings and the many jobs MA assigns her feel like pressure. Would be happier if could just baby-sit every now and then, like she did on Long Island. Then could devote more time to school and soccer or have free, unscheduled time.

Here's the scary thing.

I know exactly what she means. Just am not prepared to give up BSC. Was best thing I ever did. Can't discard it like used Kleenex. Thought of giving it up makes stomach grow cold. Awful.

On to more pleasant thoughts. Will be SO happy to see MA again. And Stacey and Claud and everyone. Just a few more days and we'll all be together. What a month has been. MA not moving — excellent, excellent news — and Cl. and St. will surely have adventures to relate.

Back to less pleasant thoughts. How are MA, St., Cl., and I going to run BSC by selves? Will have Shannon to help out every now and then, I know, but seems almost impossible. How can 5 of us do what 9 of us could just barely do?

Must turn off these horrid thoughts or will never go to sleep, and want to enjoy last days of camp.

(But am very, very worried.)

❀ Stacey

Friday

Dear Claud,

I'm on the train again. I'll be mailing this card to your house from the Stoneybrook train station. Dad, Samantha, and Ethan all came to Grand Central to see me off. I cried when I had to say good-bye. As an amusing little joke, Dad said, "Well, Samantha and I have reached a decision." (My heart jumped to my throat.) "Our decision is to wait another month before we discuss the topic again. We're going to take things very slowly."

Ha-ha. Give me a heart attack.

See you soon!

Love,
    Stacey

❋ Claudia

Friday

Dear Stacey,
We're are on are way home. This morning I said goodbye lobsters and lobstar traps, goodbye cliffs and seales, goodbye fog and mist and ocean smells, good-bye ferrys, goodbye library and lighthouse. I said my hardest good-bye yesterday. I said goodbye to Rachael. We both cried a little.

This morning I said goodbye island.

Then I said I will be back again next summer, and next summer, and the summer after that and after that.

Love,
Claudia

❀ Mary Anne

Dear diary,

Hi. Me again. It's funny. Now that my life has calmed down I don't feel so frantic about writing in you anymore. I still turn to you each and every night, but only because I want to, not because I feel I HAVE to, not because I feel that if I don't write about what happened during the day I'll explode.

So. I'm on my way back to Bradford Court. Who would have guessed? I have so many memories from that street, a lifetime of memories. When our house burned down, I lost lots of memories. Now I'm regaining some others. Maybe, in life, things do sort of even out in the end.

Of course, things won't be the same as they were

when Dad and I lived in our old house. Kristy won't be next door; the Hobarts are there instead. And we won't even be next door to the Hobarts but across the street in the Goldmans' house. When I was little, I used to be able to look out my bedroom window and into Kristy's. We would signal to each other with flashlights. I wonder if Claud and I will do that. Or are we just too grown-up?

Still, I'll be back on my old street. I'll be able to step out of the Goldmans' front door and think, There's where Kristy and I hid from Claudia the time we played that mean trick on her in second grade. There's my front stoop where I used to sit and wait for Dad to come home from work. There's the tree I was so afraid to climb. There's the little patch of daffodils that Mimi helped me plant.

I'll be in heaven.

That is, if I can ever decide what to do about Logan.

Kristy

August 1

It's the end of a very long day.

I came upstairs to my room after dinner, planning to relax by rereading this journal from the beginning, which I have just finished doing. Now it all seems so frivolous, as if I weren't taking it seriously. It was fun to read, but . . . I don't know. I think maybe I'll write this last entry here and then start a new journal tomorrow, even though this notebook is half blank. I think I have come to a good stopping place in my life, a place at which I'll end one thing and begin another.

I haven't written anything since Friday, so must back up in order to relate all that has happened.

Well . . . July is over. Claudia and Stacey and I

are back in Stoneybrook. Stacey came home on Friday, and Claud and I got back yesterday. The very first thing I did when I ran through our front door (after I yelled to Watson that no, I was not going to just leave my trunk sitting in the hall) was dash to the phone and call Mary Anne.

"Hey! You're back!" she cried. "How was Parents' Day?"

"Great! Have you found a house yet?"

"Oh, I guess you didn't get my last letter. You won't believe this! We're going to rent the Goldmans' house — NEXT DOOR TO CLAUDIA! And we're going to renovate our barn!"

Then Mary Anne dropped a bombshell. She has decided she must *seriously* consider breaking up with Logan. For good. Not like in that wimpy way she broke up with him the last time, the time that didn't take. The only thing is that she and Logan haven't spoken since their disastrous dinner. How do you break up with someone you never see?

When Mary Anne and I got off the phone I called Claudia, then Stacey. Everyone had so much to say, and we all missed each other so much that the four of us decided to get together today.

So this afternoon we sat in my room with the air

conditioner blasting. We ate chips and drank sodas and iced tea.

"Hey, you guys," said Claud at one point. She was sitting on the edge of my bed, braiding Stacey's hair, while Stacey sat on the floor at her feet. Mary Anne was lying on the bed, leaning against my reading pillow, flipping through a copy of *People*. I was sitting at my desk, tipping so far backward in my chair that Mary Anne was just inches away from telling me I was going to fall.

"Yeah?" said Stace.

"Did you ever think I'd want to move to an island?"

"You really want to move to Monhegan?" asked Mary Anne.

"One day. Definitely."

I looked around at my friends. "Hey, do you realize we are the original members of the Baby-sitters Club?" I said. "We are the ones who started it all."

"Think of everything that's happened since then," said Stacey.

"I have been. It's practically all I thought about while I was at camp."

"Really?" asked Mary Anne.

"Well, no. But I thought about it a lot."

From her spot on the bed Claud began to look uncomfortable.

"What's wrong?" I asked her.

She cleared her throat and stopped braiding Stacey's hair. "Well, it's just that I had such a great time taking Rachael's class on Monhegan. And having so much time for nothing but drawing and painting. Well . . . I began to think that I'd really like to have that luxury more often."

"Can't you?" I asked.

"Not really. Not with homework and baby-sitting and club meetings."

"You sound like Abby," I said. Then Stacey began to look uncomfortable. "What," I said crabbily.

"I was kind of thinking that I might like to have more time to go into the city. I don't know what's going to happen with Dad and Samantha, but I want to be able to watch the show. Also, the math club is going to expand next year. More meetings. More competitions."

I sighed. "What are you saying?"

"I'm saying that I don't really know how I can do all those things and continue to baby-sit as much as usual. Plus, sometimes it's hard to get to BSC meetings after math club meetings."

I glanced at Mary Anne, who had put down her magazine and was now staring at the rest of us, looking troubled. I waited for her to say how upset she was by all this, that there had been too many changes in her life recently. Instead, she said, "You know, renovating the barn is going to be an enormous job. I'm probably going to have to help Dad and Sharon quite a bit this year. I wasn't sure how to cram that in with sitting and homework and everything."

By now, Claud, Stacey, and Mary Anne were all looking at me nervously. I knew they expected me to explode. In fact, *I* expected me to explode. Instead, I heard myself saying, "Well, I guess I can understand. Lately I've been feeling just way too busy. I have homework and softball and Kristy's Krushers. Sometimes all I want is a little *free* time."

"I wonder how Shannon is feeling about the Baby-sitters Club these days," said Stacey.

We decided to call her. I can't say I was surprised to hear Shannon say pretty much the same things we'd just been saying. "In fact," she went on, "I've been trying to figure out how to tell you that I don't even think I'll have time to be an associate member of the BSC once school starts."

A few minutes later I hung up the phone. I looked at my friends. "It's just the four of us now," I said to them. "The original four." I could feel tears spring to my eyes.

"You know we won't be able to run the club the way it's been running," said Mary Anne gently. "There's just no way. We can't handle all the jobs. We could barely do it after Mallory left."

"I know."

"And the truth is," added Claudia, "we don't *want* to be as busy as we were last year."

"I know," I said again. And one of the tears escaped from my eye and ran down my cheek.

Stacey knelt beside me and wiped the tear away. "Kristy?"

"I'm okay. I know it's time to change the club. It's the right thing for all of us. Even for me. It's just . . . sad. It was a really, really good thing, and I hate to see it end."

"It's not going to end," said Stacey. "I think we should just cut back. We won't look for new clients. And we'll take fewer sitting jobs but not stop sitting altogether."

"Maybe we could meet just once or twice a week," I added.

"Perfect," said Claud.

"Really?" I asked. "Does this feel right to you guys?"

"Does it feel right to you?" asked Mary Anne.

I nodded.

"Then I think it's the right thing to do."

"Me too," said Claudia and Stacey at the same time.

And so this whole big huge chapter of my life is drawing to a close. I wonder what I'll be when I'm no longer the president of the Baby-sitters Club, when I'm just a regular kid who baby-sits. Will I still be me, Kristy Thomas?

I don't know, but I'll find out. And I'll record it all in my next journal as I begin my new life.

L. GODWIN

Ann M. Martin

About the Author

ANN MATTHEWS MARTIN was born on August 12, 1955. She grew up in Princeton, NJ, with her parents and her younger sister, Jane.

Although Ann used to be a teacher and then an editor of children's books, she's now a full-time writer. She gets ideas for her books from many different places. Some are based on personal experiences. Others are based on childhood memories and feelings. Many are written about contemporary problems or events.

All of Ann's characters, even the members of the Baby-sitters Club, are made up. (So is Stoneybrook.) But many of her characters are based on real people. Sometimes Ann names her characters after people she knows; other times she chooses names she likes.

In addition to the Baby-sitters Club books, Ann Martin has written many other books for children. Her favorite is *Ten Kids, No Pets* because she loves big families and she loves animals. Her favorite BSC book is *Kristy's Big Day*. (Kristy is her favorite baby-sitter.)

Ann M. Martin now lives in New York with her cats, Gussie, Woody, and Willy, and her dog, Sadie. Her hobbies include reading, sewing, and needlework — especially making clothes for children.

Look for #1

KRISTY'S BIG NEWS

"What is it?" I blurted out. I pushed my chair back and stood up. I couldn't think. My father never, *ever* calls us. Never. In fact, I've only seen him a handful of times since he left, including once completely by chance at a ball game in California.

"Kristy?" my mother said in a gentle voice.

"Go on," Watson said. "Why don't you use the extension in my office?"

I nodded. I turned toward Watson's office, glad to have a little time to collect myself.

I hesitated a long moment before picking up the phone. This was a clear sign that I was rattled. Any of my friends will tell you that I do *not* hesitate often.

I picked up the phone, pressed it to my ear, and said, "Hello?"

"Kristy!" My father's voice boomed over the line as if we were old buddies. "Is that you?"

"Yes," I said. "Uh, hi. How are you?"

"Oh, fine, fine. Better than fine. Excellent, in fact." My father sounded nervous — and way too cheerful. What was going on?

Charlie said, "Why are you calling?"

"Well, because I have great news. Everyone's on now, right? — Sam, Charlie?" Without waiting for an answer, my father continued, "I wanted my kids to be the first to know: I'm getting married. To Zoey. That's her name. She's great."

No one said a word. It was as if the phone connection between California and Stoneybrook had been cut off.

My father said, "Aren't you going to congratulate me?"

I heard a click. Somehow, I knew it was Charlie, hanging up the phone.

WI JUL 23 1999

Friends Baby-sitters Club *Forever*

Win a Trip to New York City!

Enter the

BSC Friends Forever New York City Getaway Sweepstakes to Visit Ann M. Martin!

Grand Prize: A New York City Getaway to visit Ann M. Martin!
100 runners-up: A signed copy of BSC Friends Forever #1: *Kristy's Big News!*
What to Do: We want to hear about your special friendships! Write a journal entry about you and your best friends and send it in!

YES! Enter me in the BSC Friends Forever New York City Getaway Sweepstakes!

Name_____ Birth Date_____

Address_____

City_____ State_____ Zip_____

Phone (_____)_____

SCHOLASTIC

BSCF199